What have we got for you in Harlequin Presents books
this month? Some of the most gorgeous men you're
ever likely to meet!

With *His Royal Love-Child,* Lucy Monroe brings
you another installment in her gripping and emotional
trilogy, ROYAL BRIDES; Prince Marcello Scorsolini
has a problem—his mistress is pregnant! Meanwhile,
in Jane Porter's sultry, sexy new story, *The Sheikh's
Disobedient Bride,* Tally is being held captive in
Sheikh Tair's harem...because he intends to tame
her! If it's a Mediterranean tycoon that you're hoping
for, Jacqueline Baird has just the guy for you in *The
Italian's Blackmailed Mistress*: Max Quintano, ruthless
in his pursuit of Sophie, whom he's determined to bed
using every means at his disposal! In Sara Craven's
Wife Against Her Will, Darcy Langton is stunned when
she finds herself engaged to businessman Joel Castille—
traded as part of a business merger! The glamour
continues with *For Revenge...Or Pleasure?*—the latest
title in our popular miniseries FOR LOVE OR MONEY,
written by Trish Morey, truly is romance on the red
carpet! If it's a classic read you're after, try *His Secretary
Mistress* by Chantelle Shaw. She pens her first sensual
and heartwarming story for the Presents line with a
tall, dark and handsome British hero, whose feisty yet
vulnerable secretary tries to keep a secret about her
private life that he won't appreciate.

Check out www.eHarlequin.com for a list of recent
Presents books! Enjoy!

Chantelle Shaw

HIS SECRETARY MISTRESS

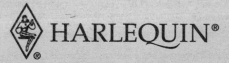

MISTRESS
TO A
MILLIONAIRE

HARLEQUIN®

TORONTO • NEW YORK • LONDON
AMSTERDAM • PARIS • SYDNEY • HAMBURG
STOCKHOLM • ATHENS • TOKYO • MILAN • MADRID
PRAGUE • WARSAW • BUDAPEST • AUCKLAND

ISBN 0-373-12546-1

HIS SECRETARY MISTRESS

First North American Publication 2006.

www.eHarlequin.com

Printed in U.S.A.

All about the author…
Chantelle Shaw

CHANTELLE SHAW lives on the Kent coast, five minutes from the sea, and does much of her thinking about the characters in her books while walking on the beach. An avid reader from an early age, school friends used to hide their books when she visited, but Chantelle would retreat into her own world, and she still writes "stories" in her head all the time. Chantelle has been blissfully married to her own tall, dark and very patient hero for over twenty years and has six children. She began to read Mills & Boon as a teenager and throughout the years of being a stay-at-home mom to her brood, she found romantic fiction helped her to stay sane! Her aim is to write books that provide an element of escapism, fun and, of course, romance for the countless women who juggle work and a homelife and who need their precious moments of "me" time. She enjoys reading and writing about strong willed, feisty women and even stronger-willed sexy heroes. Chantelle is at her happiest when writing. She is particularly inspired while cooking dinner, which unfortunately results in a lot of culinary disasters! She also loves gardening, taking her very badly behaved terrier for walks and eating chocolate (followed by more walking—at least the dog is slim!).

CHAPTER ONE

'THE traffic ahead appears to be gridlocked, Mr Morrell. Do you want me to try and turn off?'

'No, I'll walk from here. See if you can pull over, Barton.' Alex Morrell snapped his briefcase shut and punched the number of his office into his mobile phone. 'Margaret, I'm caught in traffic. Can you check that the Danson notes are complete? I'll need them for court tomorrow. Ask the temp to type up anything that's outstanding.'

There was a brief silence before his personal assistant Margaret Rivers murmured, 'She's not actually here yet, but as soon as she arrives...'

'It's ten past nine,' Alex snapped irritably, and then caught sight of the teeming London traffic and sighed. Maybe his new temporary assistant had a legitimate excuse, but it was not a promising start.

'Looks as though it might rain,' the chauffeur, Barton, noted with a glance at the heavy October sky. But Alex was impatient. He hated inactivity, and the risk of getting caught in a shower was better than sitting in the car.

He had only been walking for a few minutes when the first spots of rain turned into a deluge and he was forced to dive into the doorway of a coffee shop, colliding with a young woman who had obviously had the same idea.

'Damn! Damn! Damn!' She skidded to a halt in front of him and he flung out an arm to prevent her from falling. Hairpins scattered in all directions and her once neat chignon gave up and unravelled in a stream of amber silk around her face. 'If only I'd obeyed *Ten Tips on How to Survive Your First Day* before I set out this morning,' she said miserably, waving a bedraggled magazine under his nose. 'Tip four is to remember an umbrella.'

'What's tip one?' he enquired, unable to tear his gaze from her face, and enormous grey eyes blinked at him solemnly, dragging him under so that he felt, quite literally, as if he was drowning.

'Ensure that you arrive in plenty of time—and I'm horribly late. Do you know, the 8.05 was cancelled for no reason? Well, no reason that I could see,' she added, and Alex felt his lips twitch.

She was beautiful—exquisitely so, he acknowledged, taken aback by his reaction to her. He had met many beautiful women in his life—indeed, he was a connoisseur of tall, lissom blondes—but there was something about this woman, the curve of her cheekbones and her full, soft mouth, that sent a jolt of unwarranted desire through his body. She was slender, and so petite that the top of her head was on a level with his chest. She looked vulnerable, but in his experience women were far tougher than they looked, and it was likely that the delicate woman staring up at him was no different.

'I'm sure your boss will understand that you have no power over London Transport,' he murmured soothingly, but she shook her head again, so that her hair flashed like a bright halo round her face.

'I wouldn't bank on it. He has high expectations of his staff, and lateness is his pet hate—or so I've heard.'

'Do you mean you haven't met him?' For a brief moment Alex considered the likelihood of coincidence and then dismissed it. His personal assistant had been responsible for selecting a temporary secretary from the agency, and Margaret had described the chosen candidate as eminently sensible.

The woman standing close to him was heartstoppingly lovely, but he doubted she had been employed for her reliability; this little one could only be described as ditzy. As if to labour the point she suddenly seemed to realise that she was standing in the arms of a complete stranger, and in her efforts to escape her hair tangled round his coat button so that she was trapped.

'Wait a minute.' He stilled her wriggling and was in the process of unwinding her hair when they were joined in the doorway by a crowd of people trying to escape the hailstones that were now pelting down.

The woman was squashed up close against him and he was struck by the paleness of her skin, which was almost translucent, and her velvet-grey eyes fringed by gold-tipped lashes. There was something innately sensual about the fact that she wore no make-up apart from a hint of pale pink gloss that emphasised the fullness of her lips. Her hair smelled of lemons and rain, an earthy combination, and he fought a sudden urge to wind his fingers into the silky strands.

Could the morning get any worse? Jenna wondered. As if the public transport system hadn't been bad enough, she now faced arriving at the office on her first day looking like a drowned rat.

'I'm so sorry,' she mumbled, as the throng of people squeezed further back into the doorway, pushing her further into the stranger's arms. He towered over her, and she craned her neck to look at his face, instantly hit by a wave of attraction that sent shock waves through her body. He was gorgeous, with black hair cropped close to his head, a lean, angular face, and a wide mouth that promised heaven. His eyes were dark, almost navy in colour beneath heavy black brows, and as she stared at him he smiled, and her heart flipped in her chest.

'No problem,' he assured her, his voice rich and dark. 'It's obviously a popular doorway.'

'I must go,' Jenna muttered distractedly, dragging her gaze from him to the storm outside. Hailstones were still thundering down, and she quailed at the thought of braving them, but at this rate she would be sacked from her new job before she had even arrived.

'You can't possibly go out in that,' the man said equably, but she sensed the resolution beneath his tone and had the feeling that he would drag her physically back under the shelter should she attempt to leave.

It was all right for him, she thought, irritated by the way he continued to hold her arm, as if she was a small child in need of restraint. He didn't look like a man whose life depended on him arriving at work on time. With his exceptional height and stunning looks he had the appearance of someone who had stepped from the pages of a society magazine, but there was something about him, an air of quiet authority, that made a mockery of that idea. He must be a businessman of some sort, she surmised, and a successful one at that, for even her untutored eye could recognise the quality and superb cut of his overcoat. He was urbane, sophisticated, and from the gentle amusement in his eyes she realised that he was well aware of his affect on her.

Skin prickling with embarrassment, she dragged her eyes from his face, and as she stared down at the floor she spied the ladder in her tights.

'Someone up there really doesn't like me,' she wailed despairingly, and his gaze dropped to her legs. 'Tip five is to always carry a spare pair of tights.' She was babbling like an idiot, she realised, transfixed by the way his mouth had curved into a wide smile. She was having the morning from hell—and falling into the arms of the sexiest man she had ever met was not helping!

His eyes travelled the length of her legs, skimmed her hips and settled on her breasts, and as she felt them swell and tighten she was grateful for the protection of her jacket.

'So tell me, why have you accepted a job when you don't like the sound of the boss, and haven't even met him?' he asked curiously.

'Money,' Jenna informed him bluntly, 'lots of it. I'd work for the devil if he paid the salary I've been offered.'

Was that a look of disdain that crossed his face? If he knew the size of her mortgage he might be more under-standing, she thought grimly. She doubted he had ever had to juggle his finances to such an extreme that it was a choice between paying the bills and eating. He was rich and pampered, she decided. His clothes, his general air, exuded extreme wealth, and standing beside him in her cheap suit she felt shabby and unsophisticated. With an impatient wriggle she shrugged out of his hold and peered past the crowd to see the rain still lashing the pavement.

'I can't stay here all day,' she announced firmly. 'Do you know if there are any shops nearby? I need to buy another pair of tights.'

'Further down this road,' the man informed her. 'Why don't you phone your work and explain that you've been delayed?'

'I don't have the number,' Jenna admitted. 'It was in the memory of my phone, but somehow I erased it. Don't you dare laugh,' she warned, noting the flash of amuse-ment in his eyes as he tried to hide his smile.

She was just as he had guessed, he decided. A scatter-brained miniature Venus. But at that moment another blast of icy rain sent the crowd sheltering in the doorway surging inwards, and as she pressed up close against him he caught the drift of her perfume, a light, fresh fragrance that stirred his senses. Stirred rather more than his senses, he acknowledged.

This was ridiculous—to be so aroused at nine-thirty on a Monday morning. He had been too long without a lover, he decided grimly. At thirty-eight he was no longer at the mercy of his hormones. His days, or rather nights, with a variety of girlfriends were past, and he had certainly become more selective in his choice of lovers. But there was a huge difference between selective and celibate, and just lately he had definitely veered towards the latter. Work had become his all-consuming mistress; perhaps his body was simply reminding him that it had other needs. 'Let me buy you a coffee,' he offered as the shop door opened and the rich aroma of freshly ground beans assailed his senses. 'You can phone Directory Enquiries for the number of your office. You're late now anyway,' he added persuasively. 'Another five minutes can't harm.'

For a few seconds Jenna was tempted to throw off the weight of responsibility that had hung on her shoulders for the last three years. She stared at the stranger and her heart began a slow, thunderous beat in her chest. It wasn't just coffee he was offering, she acknowledged. The invitation was in his eyes, in the sensual curve of his mouth, and for an infinitesimal second she imagined his kiss, the feel of his lips on her neck, sliding lower to linger in the hollow between her breasts.

'I can't,' she said thickly. 'Thank you, but I can't. I'm sorry.'

She didn't know how long she stood, trapped in a haze of awareness that she could see mirrored in his eyes, but suddenly she realised that the crowd in the doorway had moved. The rain had stopped, and in the street pale sunshine danced across the puddles.

'Well, it was nice to have met you,' she said lamely as she stepped back from him, and found to her disgust that she was unable to drag her eyes from his face.

She didn't want to leave him, didn't want to walk away, knowing that she would never see him again, and she fought the urge to throw herself at him. It was only the thought of his embarrassment, let alone hers, which stopped her, and with another awkward smile she stepped into the street.

'I have to remember the way to the office block yet, and I have a terrible sense of direction.'

Alex watched her go, consumed by a fierce compulsion to follow her, pull her into his arms and kiss her delectable mouth. What was the matter with him? he thought irritably. He hadn't felt this hungry for a woman in a long time—and he didn't like it. He liked his life to be well ordered and controlled. There was no place in his schedule for sex with a scatty redhead, and he ignored the dull ache in his gut with ruthless tenacity as he strode towards his office.

'I can't understand it,' Margaret fretted when Alex entered his office to discover that the temporary secretary still hadn't shown up. 'She seemed so keen to take the job, and really she was so…' Margaret paused, and then said emphatically, 'Nice. I suppose I'd better get on to the agency,' she continued, and Alex glanced at her downcast face and sighed.

Margaret had been very enthusiastic about the young woman she had hired, and he had been happy to leave the decision to her, trusting her judgement implicitly. It seemed as though, for once, Margaret had been proved wrong.

'I'll give it until ten o'clock and then phone them myself. You'd better go if you're going to make John's appointment on time.'

'Perhaps something has happened—an accident, maybe,' Margaret said worriedly, but then her face brightened. 'You did say the traffic was particularly heavy this morning, I expect she's caught in a jam.'

Personally, Alex did not share his personal assistant's optimism that the temp would turn up. He hated having to rely on an agency for staff, but his secretarial assistant had inconveniently given birth to her baby two months early, and thrown his usually well-ordered office into chaos. It was Margaret who had suffered most; he had a particularly heavy workload of cases and the two previous temporary secretaries sent by the agency had been absolutely useless. Rather than rely on the agency's choice again, he had instructed Margaret to interview the next candidates, and he knew she would be deeply disappointed if her choice proved to be a mistake.

'I'll probably be out for most of the day,' Margaret said apologetically as she gathered up her coat and handbag. 'I imagine we'll have a long wait for the consultant.'

'Don't worry about it,' Alex advised gently. 'The most important thing is for John's condition to be assessed.'

He felt a deep sympathy for his PA; Margaret had worked for him for ten years, and had encouraged and supported him when he was a young man trying to prove his worth as a criminal lawyer in his father's law firm. Morrell and Partners had built up a reputation as one of the country's leading law firms, and Lionel Morrell's son had come under intense pressure to demonstrate that he was a creditable successor to his father. Now in her fifties, Margaret had been looking forward to early retirement with her husband, but over the last year John had experienced increasing memory loss, and, tragically, had been diagnosed as suffering from the early signs of dementia. After thirty years of marriage Margaret was devoted to her husband, and determined to stand by him, but in a bleak moment had confided to Alex that sometimes her job was the only thing that lifted her spirits.

He certainly did not want to add to Margaret's problems, Alex thought grimly. Another five minutes and he would phone the temp agency himself.

Jenna purchased a new pair of tights from a corner shop and hurried along the street as quickly as her new stiletto heels and the blister on her heel would allow. She was hot and flustered, and so intent on reaching her destination that she barely noticed the cyclist until he rode up onto the pavement. There were dozens of bicycles weaving their way through the London traffic, even the cyclist's black balaclava didn't strike her as particularly odd, and she was stunned when he suddenly screeched to a halt by a woman on the pavement and wrenched her handbag from her grasp.

For a few seconds Jenna was rooted to the spot, unable to take in what she had just witnessed, but as the woman cried out she followed a basic instinct and ran towards the cyclist. 'How dare you?' she screamed, outrage making her oblivious to the danger as she threw herself in the cyclist's path and snatched the bag.

'Get off me, bitch.' His voice was muffled through his balaclava, but the cyclist's aggression was obvious, and he quickly pushed Jenna out of his path and sped off, before any of the other pedestrians who had witnessed the scene could intervene.

At little more than five feet tall, Jenna was a light-weight, and the cyclist had used all his strength, so she literally flew through the air and met a concrete bollard with a resounding thud, her shoulder taking the force of the blow.

'Oh, God, are you okay? Have you hit your head?' The woman's hands were shaking as she stooped over Jenna. 'I can't believe you did that. I can't believe *he* did that. Do you need an ambulance?'

'No! I'm fine, really. Just a bit winded.'

Jenna was unable to disguise her panic at the thought of an ambulance. She really didn't have time for any further delays, she thought frantically, and she pinned a smile on her face, ignored the screaming pain in her shoulder and scrambled to her feet.

'Here's your bag,' she said belatedly, holding out the handbag to the woman, who shook her head disbelievingly.

'You read about these things, but I never thought...'

A curious crowd of onlookers had joined them, and Jenna smiled faintly at an elderly man who'd come to help. 'I've called the police. That was very brave of you, my dear; stupid, but brave.'

'I really must go,' Jenna said to the woman, with a hint of desperation in her voice. 'I'm late for work; I don't have time to wait for the police.'

'But you're hurt,' the woman began, and then paused, aware of the anxiety in Jenna's eyes. 'But of course you must do as you think best. Thank you for your help. Write down your name and where you work, should the police want to talk to you—although I don't suppose they'll bother. It's not as if anyone has been killed.'

'More through luck than judgement,' the older man commented dourly.

But Jenna was already hurrying on, and reaction would not set in until later.

The office block was an imposing building, the huge sheets of tinted windows glinting like copper in the autumn sunshine. The interior was a picture of discreet elegance, only the most flourishing businesses could afford to rent offices here, and Jenna was horribly aware of her laddered tights and damp skirt as she crossed the marble foyer.

As the lift carried her up to the top floor she was beset with nerves, not aided by the fact that she was now almost an hour late. She could do this, she told herself. She had excellent secretarial skills, and additional studying at college had given her the necessary qualifications for a legal secretary. Her part-time job with a small firm of solicitors had been a good learning curve, and she was more than capable of facing this new challenge head on.

Even so, her palms felt damp, her mouth dry when she introduced herself to the impeccably dressed receptionist, and was directed along the passage, a hasty glance at her watch revealing that she really had no time to pop into the cloakroom and change her tights.

Margaret Rivers was not at her desk when Jenna pushed open the door to a large open-plan office that commanded breathtaking views across the city.

'Hello, I'm Jenna Deane, from Bale's employment agency.'

At her interview she had briefly met the woman sitting at a desk at the furthest end of the room, and Katrin Jefferstone had not struck her as particularly friendly. She was tall, and whippet thin, her slenderness emphasised by the stark elegance of her black suit. Her black hair was cut into a severe bob that showed off razor-sharp cheekbones, her crisp, white shirt and scarlet lipstick the ultimate in chic sophistication.

'Goodness, you've finally arrived.' Finely plucked eyebrows disappeared beneath her fringe as the woman surveyed Jenna with barely concealed contempt, and Jenna felt her confidence trickle down to her toes. 'You'd better go straight in. We've been expecting you for the past hour.'

Taking a deep breath, Jenna pushed open the door to the inner office. 'Good morning, Mr Morrell. I'm Jenna Deane from the…' She tailed to a confused halt as the figure with his back to the door swung round on his chair.

It was a morning like no other, Jenna decided, instantly recognising the man she had met in the coffee shop doorway. He had discarded his overcoat, and his navy shirt echoed the colour of his eyes, the fine silk skimming his broad chest so that she was made aware of impressive muscle definition.

'I don't understand,' she said huskily, as realisation slowly dawned. This man, this virile, sexy man, was Alexander Morrell. He was definitely not the middle-aged, balding lawyer she had imagined her new boss to be.

'Out of interest,' Alex drawled, 'we parted company over half an hour ago, and it took me less than five minutes to reach the office. Where did you go for a new pair of tights? Scotland?'

Jenna felt the first stirrings of temper at his sarcasm, the shock of the attack, coupled with her surprise at the identity of her new boss, making her feel sick and shaky. 'I was mugged,' she said slowly. 'At least I wasn't—a woman on the pavement in front of me had her handbag snatched by a cyclist. He was wearing a balaclava,' she added, as if the information would explain everything. 'I couldn't see his face.'

'Perhaps he was working undercover?' Alex suggested dryly, his tone plainly skeptical, and Jenna felt hot colour flood her cheeks.

'You don't believe me?' Suddenly she was at boiling point. The cyclist had been the lowest of the low, but this man, with his sardonic smile and barely concealed cynicism, was the bitter end. The fact that he looked utterly gorgeous and made her feel like a self-conscious teenager only added fuel to her anger. 'I'm not in the habit of lying, Mr Morrell, but obviously I'm wasting my time here. I'll inform the employment agency that you decided I was unsuitable.'

'I may well decide that you're unsuitable, but I'll do it in my own time—which, I might add, is extremely valuable.'

Gone was the urbane charmer from the coffee shop, in his place a hard-faced criminal lawyer whose ruthlessness in the courts was legendary. His arrogance set her teeth on edge.

'I've already wasted an hour this morning, and I don't have time to run through the niceties of office politics with you now. There's a notepad on the desk. I assume you can take notes in shorthand?'

Jenna bit back a retort and seethed silently. She needed this job, she reminded herself. This was her way out of the mountain of debts that had hung over her since Lee had left; her chance to forge a better life. Before she had known his true identity, she had told Alex Morrell that she would work for the devil for the right price; it seemed as though her flippant remark was about to come true.

'Were you injured by this mystery mugger?' Alex could not quite hide his incredulity.

In all honesty he didn't know what to believe, but a career spent weeding out the truth from a web of lies had taught him that people were prepared to invent the most fantastic stories to defend themselves. He would have respected Jenna Deane more if she had simply explained that she had got lost, which was a far more likely reason for her lateness; she had admitted that she had a terrible sense of direction. He was fortunate enough not to need the services of public transport, but he was a fair man, and he could sympathise with anyone who was dependent on the notoriously unreliable train network. Miss Deane appeared windswept, but had no injuries as far as he could see, and her tale of having witnessed a mugging seemed fantastical to say the least. However, the law decreed that everyone was presumed innocent until found guilty, and he glanced at her enquiringly, prepared to be convinced.

'I'm fine, thanks,' Jenna snapped, throwing him a look of acute dislike. And to think she had thought this man fanciable! In all honesty that air of raw sexiness seemed even more intense in the confines of the office, but there was no way she would let him see that he captivated her.

'Take five minutes to tidy yourself up,' Alex advised coolly, unfazed by the storm he could see brewing in her grey eyes.

She suddenly looked very fragile, a small, forlorn figure in her rumpled suit, her red-gold hair falling in a tangle around her face. He had been unable to banish her from his mind, could hardly credit that he had been prepared to throw his tight schedule into disarray simply so that he could buy her coffee, and he could not shake off the faint disappointment that she had refused his offer.

So this was Margaret's choice, he mused. Jenna Deane would be his secretarial assistant while Pippa took six months' maternity leave. And as he flipped open the case

notes on his desk he could not dispel a frisson of antici-
pation.

Jenna felt like a recalcitrant child, sent to the cloakroom
to tidy herself up, as Alex had so tactfully put it, but one
glance in the mirror brought a gasp of dismay as she discovered just what a mess she looked. Her skirt and jacket
were inexpensive, and looked decidedly limp after a soak-
ing in the rain, but at least she was able to change out of
her laddered tights.

Her hair had been cut into a shoulder-length bob, so fine
and silky that it was difficult to put up, but she jammed a
handful of pins into her chignon and prayed that it would
stay intact. With a dash of pale lipgloss she was ready to
face Alex Morrell once more and she determined that she
would not allow him to intimidate her, holding her head
high as she pushed open the door to his office. The aroma
of freshly brewed coffee assailed her, and as she walked
across the room Alex placed a mug on the desk.

'Help yourself to cream and sugar,' he offered, adding
neither to his own mug, and she sank into the chair op-
posite him with a grateful sigh. The caffeine was a welcome boost, and it was only then that she acknowledged
how frightening the scene on the street had been.

Her shoulder throbbed, the pain running up her neck so
that it was difficult to turn her head, but Alex was studying her with quiet intensity, as if summing her up, and
she refused to make a fuss about an incident he didn't
even believe had occurred. It was galling that he should
think she had been lying. She prided herself on being
reliable and trustworthy, and as she picked up the notepad
she flashed him a glance.

'There is just one thing,' she murmured, and his brows
rose enquiringly.

'What?'

'Well, when we were sheltering from the rain and I told you that I was late, you were late too.'

Alex sat back in his chair and surveyed her in silence for several minutes, until she was squirming and wishing she'd kept quiet. He was not used to his actions being questioned, but she had sounded so indignant that he had struggled to prevent his lips from twitching.

'I'd been up since six and already put in a couple of hours' work on the computer before I left home. Being the boss does give me certain privileges. You were just late.'

His tone was amiable, but she sensed that he did not expect to argue the point any further and she bit her lip in impotent annoyance. She had also been up at dawn, had made breakfast, packed her small daughter's bag ready for day nursery, put the washing on, fed the cat, and panicked over the fact that there were only some very tired-looking sausages in the fridge for dinner that night. It was a miracle she had made it to the station on time, and the unjustness of her train being cancelled still rankled. As to the mugging, she had to admit that it did sound far-fetched, but she hated to be labelled a liar—especially, for some reason, by this man.

'If you're ready, we'll start.' Alex's voice broke into her thoughts and she held her pencil poised, ignoring the sharp pain that shot down her arm as he started to dictate.

He was testing her, she decided, when at last he stopped talking and she was able to rest her aching wrist. It was impossible to believe that he covered such a huge volume of work ordinarily, or dictated so fast. Her pencil had literally flown over the paper, and she was thankful for her excellent shorthand skills. If his intention had been to prove that she was unsuitable for the job he would be disappointed, she thought smugly, and she smiled at him as professionally as she could across the desk.

'Will that be all, Mr Morrell?'

'For now. And make it Alex. I prefer informality in my office. I'd like those letters ready before lunch, they need to catch the afternoon post. Thank you.'

He barely lifted his gaze from his computer screen and, realising that she had been dismissed, Jenna returned to the central office, wondering what had happened to Margaret Rivers. She could do with an ally, she thought wryly as she smiled tentatively at Katrin and received a cool stare in response. She had taken an instant liking to Margaret, who had interviewed her with the explanation that the senior partner of the law firm, Alex Morrell, was busy in court.

'The two previous secretaries the agency sent proved to be unsuitable,' Margaret had told her, and Jenna had been unable to hide her surprise. Bale's employment agency specialised in supplying first-class secretarial staff—she had been lucky that they had deemed her suitable for their books—and if the other secretaries had not been good enough for Morrell and Partners, there seemed little hope for her.

'Can I ask what was wrong with them?' she had queried tentatively, and Margaret had smiled warmly at her.

'The first one made it plain that she was more interested in Alex Morrell than work,' she said. 'Really it was quite embarrassing; she was all over him—blatant as anything. It happens, of course. Alex is a very wealthy and successful man, but he likes to keep work and play separate, and Lydia made no secret that she wanted to play. The second girl was nice, and she had excellent qualifications, but she had childcare problems. Apparently her nanny had walked out and she forever had to dash off early or arrived late. Alex is a stickler for punctuality,' Margaret had confided. 'Poor Karen. I felt sorry for her, but once she even brought the baby into the office. Alex was not impressed.'

There had been an awkward pause; Margaret had obviously felt uncomfortable as she continued, 'The position of secretarial assistant is quite demanding. My husband is unwell, and although I am Alex's personal assistant, I can't work late or travel to meetings like I used to. Alex needs someone who doesn't have too many other commitments, like children.' Margaret's embarrassment had been tangible, and she had grimaced before adding, 'Of course it's not politically correct to mention it, but children and pregnancy can be rather awkward for a busy firm like Morrell and Partners, as Pippa's unexpectedly early maternity leave proves. Alex was hugely sympathetic, and fortunately Pippa's tiny baby is thriving, but it has all been quite difficult. Would you find that level of commitment a problem?' Margaret had queried, her gaze straying to Jenna's midriff, and Jenna had laughed and assured the older woman that she had no intention of having a baby.

She had neatly sidestepped the issue of any existing children, but all the way home she had worried about Maisie. She was committed to the hilt, she had brooded. Her daughter would be four in a couple of months; old enough to settle happily at the day nursery, the supervisor had assured her. But in Jenna's eyes Maisie was just a baby, and the thought of leaving her all day tore at her heart. She was lucky that she could rely on her wonderful neighbours, who had promised to care for Maisie whenever necessary. Nora and Charlie adored Maisie, and had adopted her as their surrogate grandchild, filling the void left by their own childlessness. Without them she could not have even contemplated the job with Morrell and

Partners, Jenna had conceded. But it did little to assuage the guilt that she was somehow abandoning her daughter.

She was here now, Jenna thought as she switched on her computer and began to transcribe the morning's work. She had entered the lion's den and made such a bad first impression she would almost certainly be deemed as unsuitable as her predecessors.

For Maisie's sake she needed this job. The salary offered was better than any other job she had seen advertised, and if Alex Morrell had an aversion to working mothers then keeping quiet about her little daughter was a necessity—at least until she had proved her worth.

CHAPTER TWO

IT WAS one o'clock before Jenna looked up from her computer screen, her aching shoulder vying for attention with her rumbling stomach. She had never worked so hard in her life, had dealt with numerous phone calls in between typing, and felt a certain satisfaction that she had finished all that Alex had requested on time. Of the man himself she had seen no sign, her conversations with him brief and to the point as she put through calls or relayed messages.

Now, as she stretched and glanced around the large open-plan office, she felt a pang of longing for the homely office of Philips and Co, the small firm of solicitors where she had previously worked. Gone were the days of a mid-morning cup of tea and a cake, lunch with her friend Claire, and the chance to pop into the supermarket or window-shop. The Morrell and Partners offices were in the heart of the city and no way did she have the clothes or the money to have lunch in one of the exclusive wine bars. It was lucky she had brought her lunch with her, she thought; she was so hungry that even the limp sandwich in the bottom of her bag would be welcome.

At the far end of the room was a door leading to the office of the other senior partner, Charles Metcalf, and Jenna turned away from the view of London to speak to Charles's secretary—Katrin Jefferstone. 'Do you think it's okay if I go to lunch?' she queried. 'Alex is on the phone and asked not to be disturbed.'

'Go when you want,' Katrin answered in a bored tone,

her gaze flicking over Jenna's cheap suit with scathing dismissal. 'I'll let Alex know.'

With a thankful sigh Jenna made her escape, unaware that Alex had been watching her for much of the morning through the tinted glass that separated the offices. Minutes later he cut his call and strolled into the central office.

'Where's Jenna?'

'She said something about going to lunch. I did suggest that she check with you first, but…' Katrin tailed off and shrugged her shoulders in a gesture of resignation. 'Oh, dear, Alex. Not another useless temp?'

'We'll see,' Alex murmured in a non-committal voice as he glanced through the pile of correspondence Jenna had left for him to sign.

There was no problem with her diligence, he mused. His eyes had strayed with irritating monotony to the figure working in the outer office, but she hadn't glanced up from her work, and his earlier reservations were subsiding. The problem was him, he acknowledged grimly. It had taken sheer determination to stop himself from strolling out to talk to her, and he had invented several reasons for doing just that, discarding them with derision—he would appear too obvious or, worse, desperate.

She wasn't even his type. His usual girlfriends were tall and elegant, and, having been blessed with wealth, looks and an innate charm, he could choose from the cream of London's socialites. So why had he spent the morning planning on taking his temporary secretary to lunch? Even worse, having missed his chance, how was he going to glean from the frighteningly efficient Katrin where Jenna had gone?

In the event it was the receptionist on the front desk who told him Jenna had asked for directions to the nearest park, and as he stepped out into the damp autumn air he was still arguing with himself over his reasons for seeking her out.

The park was a small oasis of tranquillity amidst the hubbub of the city, and as Jenna stared up through the trees she felt her tension ease. As first days went it had been a disaster, she thought dismally, although hopefully the quality of her work would meet Alex Morrell's high standards and he wouldn't dismiss her at the end of day one. She was still indignant that he hadn't believed her reason for being late, and was half tempted to tell him to stick his job, but her hot temper had always been her Achilles' heel, and at twenty-four it was time she learned to control it.

So much depended on her keeping this job; without its high salary she was in danger of losing the house, of having to uproot Maisie and move away from everything that was familiar to the little girl. At her interview Margaret had hinted that Pippa, the secretary on maternity leave, might possibly decide not to return to work at all, in which case the post of secretarial assistant would become permanent. Not that she could keep Maisie a secret for ever, Jenna fretted, but if she could prove to Alex that she had foolproof childcare arrangements then perhaps the fact that she had a daughter would no longer be an issue.

Did he dislike children? she wondered. Or was it simply that he had little sympathy for working mothers? Neither reason endeared him to her, so why had she been unable to dismiss his handsome face from her mind all morning? He was sex on legs, she acknowledged with a rueful smile, and it had taken sheer will-power to prevent her eyes from straying towards the dark tinted glass that separated her office from his.

'So, you decided on lunch al fresco?' A voice as cool and clear as a mountain stream trickled over her and she was unable to repress a shiver, felt goosebumps prickle her skin as she turned her head. 'Do you mind if I join you?'

He had already sat down on the bench and her tension returned with a vengeance. She wished he would go, and at the same time wanted him to stay. She needed to look at him again, although one peep was enough to send her pulse racing, and with a determined effort she dragged her eyes away and stared at the ducks on the pond.

'Help yourself,' she answered, striving to sound cool and composed, but aware that her voice was starting to sound breathless.

'I had planned on taking you to lunch, to give us a chance to get to know one another properly.'

Jenna swung round, her eyes colliding with his sapphire gaze, and she swallowed, her nerves jangling when she discovered how close he was. His hair was the colour of jet, cropped uncompromisingly short so that she noted the hard planes of his face, the classically sculpted cheek-bones and square jaw. There were laughter lines around his eyes and she longed to see him smile, for his eyes to glint with warmth when he looked at her.

'I'm sorry, I didn't realise. Do you do that with all your new staff? Take them to lunch, I mean?' she added, disconcerted by his intense appraisal.

'No,' he replied, and reached out to brush a stray lock of hair from her cheek.

The gesture was so intimate that she felt herself blush. He was too close for comfort. She was aware of the tantalising musk of his aftershave, the warmth of his breath on her skin.

'We didn't get off on the best of footings this morning,' he continued quietly, and she knew he was referring to her lateness and the unbelievable reason for it. He still considered that she had lied, she realised; she opened her mouth to protest her innocence, looked into his eyes and lost the ability to think.

'Would you like a sandwich?' she offered, frantically searching for something to say to break the silence that thrummed with electricity.

'What's in them?' he queried, glancing at the unappealing squares of white bread on her knee.

'Jam.'

His expression was faintly disbelieving as he held up his hand. 'I'll pass, thanks. I haven't eaten jam since I was a child.'

She wasn't lunching on jam sandwiches out of choice either, Jenna thought, irritated by his amusement. What had he expected? Smoked salmon? Although in fairness that was probably the sort of lunch he was used to, and she certainly couldn't reveal that she had saved the last slices of cheese for Maisie's lunch.

'I need to go shopping,' she admitted as she picked up a sandwich, but her appetite seemed to have vanished along with her peace of mind.

'There's a little bistro at the edge of the park that serves lovely food and the best lemon meringue pie,' Alex added, with another glance at her pathetic lunch. 'Shall we start afresh over something to eat? I watched you working like a demon this morning; you must be hungry.'

'You watched me?' For a second Jenna envisaged him snooping on her through some sort of spyhole, her dismay written all over her face, and he could not prevent his smile.

'The glass walls between our offices are tinted, but I can see out quite well. I hope you don't find that unsettling?'

She did, hugely, but could hardly admit it. Thank God

she hadn't drifted off into one of her daydreams, where she lost all concept of time and filled several sheets of paper with sketches. She didn't think he would be quite so friendly if he deemed her a time waster, and once again she realised that the job at Morrell and Partners was light years away from her comfortable existence at Philips and Co.

'Do you know those little gold freckles across your nose are really beautiful?'

Alex Morrell had little in common with the fatherly Mr Philips either, Jenna acknowledged, sheer panic sending her jumping to her feet. Faced with the full force of his charm she quailed.

'You must be a mind reader. I love lemon meringue pie. And I hate my freckles,' she added on an afterthought. 'I've got them everywhere.'

'Really?' She steadfastly ignored the wicked glint in his eyes, and to her relief he said no more on the subject of freckles or their whereabouts and led the way across the park to the bistro.

Alex Morrell was something else, Jenna mused as she stirred her coffee and contemplated the best lunch she had eaten in months. As if stunning good looks were not enough, he was witty, charming and fiercely intelligent, and he had entertained her with tales of past court cases and amusing incidents from his life as a barrister. All through lunch she had listened and laughed, utterly captivated, so that she'd relaxed and unknowingly lowered the barriers she had erected against him.

He had been too hard on her this morning, Alex chided himself as he watched the way she licked the last morsel of meringue from her spoon, the tip of her pink tongue a tantalising distraction from which he had difficulty dragging his gaze. She was unknowingly sexy—or perhaps knowingly, he thought with a frown. The sexuality she exuded was not lost on him, as the ache in his loins could verify, but there was an air of innocence about her that tugged at his protective streak even as he derided himself for his gullibility.

In his opinion women were by far the stronger sex, and in court they had never ceased to amaze him with their ability to lie in order to save their own skins. The jury was still out on Jenna Deane, and he could not pigeonhole her yet, but getting to know her was proving to be an interesting experience.

The autumn sunshine had disappeared when they walked back across the park, and the sudden downpour was as violent as it was unexpected.

'Tomorrow I'm going to bring an umbrella,' Jenna vowed as raindrops the size of pennies spattered her skirt for the second time that day.

'Over here—come on!' With the shower showing no sign of abating Alex caught hold of her arm, and together they scrambled for the protection of one of the few trees that still retained its leaves.

As they ran, Jenna skidded on the wet leaves underfoot and fell bodily against Alex, who braced himself against the tree trunk, taking her weight on his chest.

'I'm sorry.' Her hair had come loose again, and she stared up at him through a tangle of amber silk, the laughter dying in her throat as she caught the unguarded look in his eyes.

'This is becoming a habit,' he murmured, stroking her hair back from her face. 'A very pleasant habit, I might add.'

Was he was going to kiss her? she wondered, with the tiny part of her brain still capable of thought. His dark head lowered, seemingly in slow motion, and she felt the warmth of his breath on her cheek, could see the fine laughter lines that crinkled the corners of his eyes. Already that sensual mouth was hovering millimetres from hers, and she couldn't deny the heady excitement that swept over her. She was desperate to feel him, skin on skin.

Was it some kind of test? she wondered numbly. Margaret had said that one of the previous secretaries had been deemed unsuitable because she'd made her attraction to Alex obvious. Standing in his arms, virtually begging for him to kiss her, was being more than just obvious, but she seemed to have no control over her body. She was stunned by her reaction to him; common sense seemed to have deserted her.

Without conscious thought her lips parted, but instead of accepting her offer he drew back, his low murmur bringing her back to earth with a bump. Of course he wasn't going to kiss her! He had drawn her into his arms simply to prevent her from slipping on the leaves, and was no doubt horrified to find himself pinioned to the tree. Shame scalded her, and she jerked away from him, her cheeks on fire, unable to meet his gaze, which she was certain would reflect his sardonic amusement.

'We should head back. We've a busy afternoon ahead.'

Alex's voice cut through her mental self-flagellation and she nodded wordlessly, wondering how he could sound so calm and in control. But then he hadn't made a complete fool of himself, she reasoned miserably. If he had been setting her some sort of test she had failed spectacularly, but the idea that she might not have a job by the end of the day was almost a relief. She didn't think she could cope with Alex Morrell on a long-term basis.

She trudged beside him on the walk back through the park, determined not to look at him or speak to him unless absolutely necessary, but he too seemed lost in his thoughts and disappeared into his inner sanctum as soon as they reached the office.

Jenna was tired and emotionally drained. Her shoulder, which had ached dully all morning, was now throbbing, but she ploughed on with her work, struggling to get to grips with an unfamiliar program on her computer. Twenty futile minutes later she conceded that she would have to ask for help, and spent another ten practising the right amount of cool uninterest in her tone.

Alex wasn't working, as she'd assumed when she entered his office, but staring out over the magnificent view of London, and she wondered if he too had a penchant for daydreaming. Although from his stern expression it was not a pleasant dream. At her hesitant request for assistance he insisted on coming out to view her screen and she was achingly aware of his lean, hard body and the enticing scent of his aftershave as he leaned across her.

His instructions were concise, and when he had finished he eased back and rested a hand on her shoulder.

'Ow!' She could not prevent her cry of pain and he raised his eyebrows quizzically.

'What's the problem?'

'Nothing. It's just my shoulder. I think it must be bruised from this morning...' She tailed to a halt under his intent stare and flushed. Did he still think she was lying? Her shoulder was in agony and she certainly wasn't making it up.

'You were injured this morning? Yet you didn't think to mention it? As I remember, I asked you specifically if you'd been hurt.'

'You didn't even believe I'd been involved in an attack. As I remember you were being sarcastic, and I didn't want to make a fuss—not after arriving an hour late.'

'I would happily have believed you, had you shown any sign of distress,' he bit out, fury with himself making his tone sharp. He prided himself on his sense of justice and fair play, and all day it had niggled him that he had written her off as unreliable when she had proved patently that she was not.

This close he could see the faint shadows beneath her eyes, her skin so translucent he could trace the fine blue veins beneath the surface. She was exquisitely beautiful, as delicate as a porcelain figurine, and he had to tear his gaze from her face before he gave in to the temptation to kiss her, as he had so nearly done in the park.

'If your shoulder is still hurting five hours after the...' he hesitated fractionally '...incident, then it must need medical attention. Undo your blouse so that I can take a look.'

Jenna blinked at him indignantly. 'I'm not stripping off in the middle of the office!'

'I'm merely suggesting that you unfasten the top couple of buttons.' He gave her a withering look. 'I have seen a woman's naked shoulder before, and I promise I won't be overcome with lust.'

Was that a deliberate taunt? she wondered. A reminder that he was aware of just how much she wanted him? His face was impassive, giving no clues to his thoughts, but he was a master of disguising his emotions and his features were set in the aloof expression he usually reserved for cross-questioning.

He was so arrogant, Jenna thought furiously, her temper suddenly white-hot. 'Hold on a minute,' she snapped. 'This morning you didn't believe a word about the "incident"—your word, not mine, and now suddenly you're Dr Kildare! My shoulder's bruised; I can move it quite well, so it's not broken, and I'll see to it when I get home.'

'Fine. Get your jacket, we'll go to Casualty.'

'No!' Her arms were folded across her chest; he wouldn't have been surprised if she had stamped her foot in fury, and despite everything his lips twitched.

'It's your choice,' he said equably. 'Either I look at it or a doctor does. Take your pick.'

Her answer was to stalk into his office, her back rigid with outrage as she ripped apart the top buttons of her blouse and shrugged the material over her injured shoulder.

Already feeling bad, the sight of the huge purple bruise that covered her shoulder filled him with remorse. 'What happened, exactly? Did someone hit you?'

Jenna shook her head. 'He didn't attack me at all. As I was walking along a cyclist suddenly rode onto the pavement and snatched the handbag from the woman in front of me. I ran to help and he pushed me against a concrete bollard. But I managed to save the bag,' she added brightly.

'You bloody idiot; he might have had a weapon. What would you have done if he'd pulled out a knife? What are you, anyway? All of five feet nothing and you think you're a one-woman army!'

'I didn't think. I saw the attack and I lost my temper, okay?' In her frustration Jenna swung round to face him, remembering belatedly her open blouse and the expanse of lilac lace bra on display.

Since her parents and her brother had emigrated to New Zealand, to be near her sister, birthday and Christmas presents had been defined by their ease of packing—and she owned drawers full of pretty lingerie. This lilac bra was of such sheer lace it was almost transparent, and to her horror she felt her nipples harden, the dark peaks plainly visible through the material.

With a yelp she swung back and scrabbled with the buttons. 'Why should you care anyway?' she threw at him, and he stilled, his gaze intent as he turned her back to face him.

'You've fastened the buttons wrong,' he murmured, his fingers feather-light against the swell of her breasts as he corrected them. 'I think that hot temper of yours might lead you into real trouble some day, Jenna Deane. You seem to be a cauldron of wild emotions just waiting to boil over.'

His voice was suddenly as deep and soft as crushed velvet, and she felt a burning sensation behind her eyelids. He towered over her, so big, yet suddenly so gentle, and she fought the urge to throw herself against his chest and burst into tears.

'Hello, I'm back at last.' Margaret Rivers popped her head round the door of the office, patently unaware of the crackling tension between its occupants, and beamed as she spied Jenna. 'Mrs Deane—Jenna—I knew you wouldn't let us down. How's your first day been?'

She disappeared for a second, long enough for Alex's eyebrows to shoot upwards, his puzzlement obvious.

'*Mrs* Deane?' he queried, but Margaret was back, waving Jenna's handbag.

'Your mobile has rung several times, dear. Perhaps it's important.'

Jenna stared at the older woman blankly and then scrabbled in her bag for her phone. She recognised the number of the caller and her expression softened. Her younger brother Chris was travelling from New Zealand and had been backpacking through Europe, he must have arrived in England sooner than planned. Suddenly everything faded into insignificance; she hadn't seen her brother for two years and had missed him and the rest of her family desperately since they had emigrated.

'Chris, darling, I can't wait to see you.' There was no disguising the pleasure in her voice, the soft glow of love in her eyes, and Alex stared at her for a moment before turning to Margaret, impeccable manners demanding that he give Jenna privacy to take her call. But inside he was seething.

Jenna finished her conversation with Chris, explaining that she had left the key to her house with her neighbours and urging him to make himself at home. She would be back as soon as possible, she promised, glowing with excitement as she replaced her phone. But when she looked up she discovered that Margaret was no longer in the office and she was alone with a grim-faced Alex Morrell.

'Out of interest,' he drawled, his voice deceptively soft, 'when were you going to mention Chris?'

Jenna gave a puzzled frown. Why was it necessary for her to mention her brother at all?

'That *is* your husband's name I assume? Chris?'

He was studying her with his piercing blue eyes and the moment she met his gaze she felt herself blush. How was she going to manage working for him when she couldn't even look at him? she thought despairingly. The worst of it was he knew the effect he had on her, and presumably found it amusing. It was so humiliating. She shuddered at the idea of being known as the secretary with an outsized crush on her boss and her chin came up. She could imagine his pitying expression if she admitted that she had been divorced after just one miserable year of marriage. It would only reinforce his belief that she was a desperate man-hunter.

'Yes, Chris is my husband,' she lied. 'I assumed you

knew I was married. It's not a secret; my agency details state that I'm Mrs Deane.'

'In that case, just what were you playing at in the park?' He glared at her across the room, his eyes as dark and fathomless as pools of ink although his icy disdain was obvious. 'Of course I didn't know. I'm not in the habit of making a pass at my married staff.'

Or any of his staff, for that matter, he added silently. He had always been scrupulous about keeping his work and private life separate, and was furious with himself for a serious lack of judgement. He was furious with her too, ostensibly for not being straight with him. But if he was being honest, he acknowledged grimly, he hated the idea that she had a husband.

'I wasn't playing at anything. I don't know what you mean,' she snapped, outrage and embarrassment stoking her temper.

'Oh, come on. You were issuing me with a very definite invitation in the park. I'd love to be a fly on the wall when your husband asks you about your day,' he continued sarcastically, ignoring her furious gasp of denial. 'Will you mention that you want your boss? Or do you prefer to keep the poor sod in the dark about your extra-curricular activities?'

Jenna drummed her fingers on the desk and fought to keep a lid on her temper. 'Naturally I won't refer to an incident that I found to be frankly embarrassing.'

'Embarrassing! Oh, I see—you're suggesting that your boss placed you in an awkward situation? Why don't you have done with it and report me for sexual harassment?'

'Don't be ridiculous; I'm just trying to say that you obviously read something into the situation that wasn't there. You're very nice,' she said placatingly, 'but I certainly wasn't flirting with you. I'm a happily married woman.'

'I suppose you're now going to tell me that you're intending to produce a brood of little Deanes too?' he said through gritted teeth. Her description of him as 'nice' stung; he had never been called *nice* in his life, and his male pride was outraged at her implication that he was middle-aged and past it.

'God, no.' Jenna gave a brittle laugh and crossed her fingers behind her back. Somehow she had managed to insult him, and he was looking for a reason to dismiss her and demand that the agency send a replacement. If she admitted that she had a pre-school child she would be out of the job that was hopefully going to turn her life around. The agency would be distinctly unimpressed to learn that she had only survived one day with their most prestigious client, and would be in no hurry to find her other work, but everything depended on her ability to earn a high salary. 'I'm a committed career woman,' she informed him coolly. 'Children don't feature on my agenda.'

Alex stared at her, his expression giving nothing away—certainly not his inexplicable feeling of disappointment at her words. What was the matter with him? Maybe he was having a mid-life crisis, he thought irritably as he banished the picture of a rosy-cheeked child with hair like spun gold from his mind. He didn't even like children particularly, and it should have come as a great relief that his new secretary had no maternal urges.

The silence in the room seemed to stretch interminably, and the tap on the door caused Jenna to jump. Her eyes narrowed as she stared at Katrin, some sixth sense warning her that the other woman had been listening in on the conversation.

'The police have come for Mrs. Deane,' Katrin announced with understated calm.

'Excellent. On top of everything, I've employed the Boston Strangler.'

That was it, Jenna decided. She would rather sell her body than work one more minute for Alex Morrell. But there was no time to inform him of the fact. Two burly police officers were already towering over her, and although she knew she was the victim of a crime rather than its perpetrator, she swallowed nervously.

Despite their indomitable presence, the policemen were surprisingly gentle as they questioned her about the mugging she had witnessed, pointing out that it had been unwise to tackle the cyclist, who might have been carrying a weapon.

'A knife, a gun—you just don't know these days, Mrs Deane. It's not worth risking your life for a few valuables.'

'Absolutely,' Alex concurred, and received a venomous glare for his pains.

'I'd make an appointment with your GP to get that shoulder checked out,' one officer suggested as they stood to leave, and Jenna gave her smiling assurance that she would do so, mentally adding the white lie to the various other untruths she had uttered that day. She prided herself on her honesty, yet one day of working for Alex Morrell and she had turned fibbing into an art form.

Alex escorted the policemen out of the office and she sank into a chair feeling utterly drained. Her face was pale with misery when he returned. This latest disruption to his day was no doubt the last straw; he would never keep her on now.

'I suppose you want me to leave,' she murmured, and

he spared her a brief glance before turning his attention to his computer screen.

'Excellent idea. Go and collect your things.'

As she struggled to push her aching arm into her jacket she debated going back into his office to admit the truth— that far from being happily married and childless she was a single mother, struggling to juggle a career and care for an almost four-year-old—but it all seemed too complicated and she just wanted to go home.

'Goodbye.'

The voice from the doorway was curiously deflated, and Alex felt compassion snag his heart as he studied the small, forlorn figure. 'I'm coming with you,' he said calmly, and something flared in her eyes.

'You don't need to see me off the premises. I feel humiliated enough that everyone knows I was interviewed by the police.'

'Never mind what anyone else thinks,' he replied cheerfully, and that just about summed him up, she decided. He was confident to the point of arrogance—but then he was the boss; he didn't have to care what anyone else thought.

She half expected him to frogmarch her out of the office block, but when the lift came to a halt she discovered that they were in an underground car park.

'My car's over there.' He was already leading the way to a silver Bentley, and as they approached a uniformed chauffeur sprung out and held open the door.

'There's no need for all this. I've got a return train ticket,' she said faintly as she sank into the supple leather upholstery. 'Just drop me at the station.'

Alex ignored her and leaned forward to speak into the intercom. 'Harley Street, please, Barton.'

CHAPTER THREE

'I'M NOT getting out of the car.'

Jenna folded her arms across her chest, belligerence thrumming from every pore, and Alex fought to keep a lid on his temper. Until today he hadn't been aware that he even possessed a temper. Even when annoyed he was able to deal with issues in a calm, controlled manner, but where Jenna was concerned it seemed that any sense of control flew out of the window.

'I'll decide whether or not I need to see a doctor, and if I think it necessary I'll make an appointment with my own GP, not yours. I can't afford a private Harley Street practitioner.'

'I'm not asking you to.' Alex closed his eyes and briefly pictured newspaper headlines that screamed *Top Barrister Commits Murder.*

'Anyway,' Jenna continued stubbornly, 'the only reason we're here is so that you can appease your conscience. I told you I wasn't a liar.'

'Either you get out of the car or I'll drag you out.' Any vestige of control disappeared in a cloud of molten fury. Her husband must have the patience of a saint, Alex decided, ignoring the fact that her jibe had hit home.

There was no warmth in his eyes now, his face was a rigid mask of irritation, and Jenna realised that compliance was her only option if she was to retain any dignity. She didn't doubt for a minute that he would carry out his threat to drag her bodily from the car, and so, with her head held high, she opened the door.

'He's probably busy anyway,' she muttered as she was ushered into a plush reception area that bore scant resemblance to her own doctor's drab surgery.

'Hello, Alex. Go straight through. Guy is expecting you.' If the receptionist was surprised to see Alex leading his companion along like a badly behaved puppy she was far too discreet to mention it, and Jenna pulled her hand free and stomped into the inner office.

'Alex—good to see you. We must meet up for a game of golf; my club, Saturday?'

'Actually, I'm flying to Cannes this weekend. But another time certainly.'

'Hoping to prolong the summer, huh? And no doubt enjoy the company of some tanned blonde beauty. You need to settle down and get married, Alex.'

'Why?' Alex queried with a grin, and Guy laughed.

'There must be a good reason, but it beats me.'

Jenna hovered in the doorway, feeling superfluous. This was not her world, and it was safe to say that she wouldn't be playing golf or sunning herself in Cannes at the weekend. From the knowing glances that had passed between the two men it was obvious that Alex had a reputation—hardly surprising, considering his stunning looks, she reminded herself. But the thought left her feeling curiously flat.

'And this must be the young lady with the shoulder injury.' Guy Deverille welcomed her with a smile. 'Alex explained about the incident on your way to work this morning. Let's take a look, shall we?'

We! Jenna's gaze flitted from the doctor to Alex. No way was she going to strip off in front of Alex for the second time that day, she vowed, and Alex's lips twitched as he read her expression.

'I'll leave you to it,' he murmured, and as he headed

for the door her fingers itched to wipe the mocking smile from his face.

'I told you it was just bruised,' she berated half an hour later, as the Bentley cruised through the London streets. After ensuring that she had suffered no broken bones, Guy Deverille had given her some strong painkillers and advised her to rest her shoulder as much as possible for the next couple of days.

'So you did,' Alex agreed equably, not looking up from his laptop, and she gave up and stared moodily out of the window.

Having been spared the train journey home, she was early. She would be able to collect Maisie from the nursery, rather than her neighbour, Nora, and her heart lifted at the thought of seeing her daughter. She hated having to leave Maisie all day, and the decision to return to full-time work had been a hard one—although the bank did not share her concerns, and had only increased her mortgage on the understanding that her salary would cover the repayments.

The chauffeur parked in her tree-lined suburban street and she turned to Alex, her heart suddenly sinking. This was goodbye to her job, and quite possibly her home if she didn't find another position quickly. It was certainly goodbye to the most intriguing man she had ever met, for she doubted she would see Alex Morrell again. Somehow it seemed unlikely that they would ever move in the same social circles.

'Take tomorrow off and rest your shoulder. I expect you to be in the office at nine o'clock on Wednesday morning.' At her silence Alex spared her a brief, quizzical glance and she stared at him.

'I thought you didn't want me any more—to work for you, I mean,' she added clumsily, her cheeks flaming.

'Whatever gave you that idea?' His sarcasm grated as Jenna ran a brief resumé of the day's events in her head, and after studying her downcast face he finally took pity on her. 'It wasn't the best first day, I agree. The visit from the police was a particularly low point, but aside from various catastrophes your work was excellent, and I need a secretary. I'm sure it's going to be a pleasure working with you, Mrs Deane.'

There would be no more flirting, Jenna realized. No element of the sexual tension that had burned between them although they had both denied its existence. Now that Alex believed she was married she was deemed out of bounds, and he had no interest in her other than for her secretarial skills.

She should have felt relieved, but as she walked up the path her front door was flung open and she threw herself into Chris's arms and burst into tears.

'So, how was your day?' Chris had developed a strong accent since he had emigrated to New Zealand with their parents, four years before, and Jenna managed a watery smile as he added, 'My guess is, not good.'

'You have no idea.' Jenna sniffed, scrubbing her eyes with a tissue and stepping back to survey her kid brother—who towered over her. 'I know I sound like Mum, but you have grown!'

Chris grinned cheerfully. 'Yeah, well, it's two years since you visited New Zealand. I guess we've all changed—although you haven't grown,' he teased. 'How's that cute little niece of mine?'

'Maisie has definitely grown,' Jenna informed him. 'She's at the day nursery until half past five.'

'And you're now trying to hold down a full-time job?' Chris's smile faded. 'Mum told me that your jerk of an ex-husband won his court case. I can't believe he was awarded a percentage of the value of your house when you were only able to buy it in the first place using the money left to you by Auntie Vi.'

'That money only paid the deposit,' Jenna explained. 'The mortgage was in both our names, and technically Lee was entitled to his share. I could sell up, but by the time I've paid legal costs and everything I'll only be able to afford a small flat. I don't want to uproot Maisie; she loves the garden and her rabbit, and Nora and Charlie next door are like grandparents to her—she'd miss them terribly.'

'I know,' Chris muttered, 'but it still seems unfair on you. Lee's never contributed to Maisie's upbringing in any way, financially or emotionally, and because of him you're forced to work for some demon of a boss who makes you cry.'

'Alex Morrell isn't that bad,' Jenna lied. 'Today was my first day and it was a bit fraught, that's all. There was a lot to learn.'

The most important lesson being to keep her distance from Alex, she acknowledged silently. Chris had called him a demon, yet in all fairness she couldn't say that he was an unpleasant boss. He was demanding, with high expectations of his staff, but in return he rewarded them well, and against all the odds he had given her a second chance. It was a chance she was not going to waste. She would prove to Alex Morrell that she was as conscientious and efficient as he could possibly want, and if the only way she could do that was to avoid making eye contact with him, then so be it.

'The parents send their love.' Chris interrupted her thoughts as she entered the living room, which was strewn with his rucksack and various other packages. 'Along with masses of presents for Maisie. I'd better warn you that I've been instructed to try and persuade you to move out to New Zealand. Mum and Dad miss you.' He shrugged awkwardly. 'We all do.'

'I miss all of you too,' Jenna murmured thickly, thinking of her elderly parents, who had been looking forward to their retirement when tragedy had struck. Their eldest daughter, Faye, had emigrated to her husband's homeland of New Zealand after her marriage, but had suffered a stroke whilst giving birth to her first baby. Believing that Jenna was settled at art college, Neil and Mary Harris had moved to Auckland to help Faye in her slow recovery programme.

It had been a terrible time, Jenna recalled. She was close to her sister, and had longed to go to her, but she had just discovered that she was pregnant with Maisie. Her boyfriend Lee's promise to stand by her had seemed like a blessing at the time, and she had gratefully accepted his marriage proposal, ignoring her misgivings about the relationship in an effort to spare her parents further worry.

Unfortunately Lee had caused her nothing but worry and grief, their marriage proving to be a disaster from the very beginning. It was when she'd realised that his constant infidelity no longer hurt that she had accepted their relationship was over—although Lee's overspending and their spiralling debts hadn't helped. She had spent weeks worrying about where she could go with a young baby, and had been relieved when Lee finally walked out. The numerous credit card bills he'd left behind were a small price to pay for her freedom.

'I have thought about moving out to join you,' she admitted. 'But Mum and Dad have had enough to worry about with Faye. Any problems I have are my own fault. They warned me that Lee seemed unreliable, but I was besotted with him and wouldn't listen. Maybe if I hadn't fallen pregnant I would have seen him for what he really is, but discovering that I was expecting Maisie was a shock, and I was just so grateful when he promised to stand by me. Faye was so ill at the time,' she continued, 'and I didn't want to add to Mum and Dad's problems. And even though Faye is so much better, I still don't. I'm a grown woman now, and this is my home. I can look after myself and Maisie. I can't run back to Mum and Dad whenever things get difficult.'

'You always were a feisty little thing,' Chris said with a grin, and Jenna returned his smile.

'I'm so glad you're here,' she said softly. 'It's a great idea to have a gap year before university. How long do you think you'll stay?'

'A couple of months, if you'll have me. I need to get a job and save up before I do any more travelling—but right now isn't it time to collect Maisie? I can't wait to see her.'

It was late in the evening before Jenna finally persuaded Maisie into her bath and bed routine, and the little girl was still bubbling with the excitement of her uncle's visit when she snuggled under her duvet. She appeared quite happy after her long day at the nursery—indeed, she informed Jenna that she was now one of the 'big girls' and only babies were collected at lunchtime.

She was asleep within minutes of her head touching the pillow, and Jenna felt a surge of adoration for her little girl. Maisie had always been small for her age and had lost her baby chubbiness, her face as delicate as one of the fairies that adorned her bedroom wall. She had inherited Jenna's grey eyes and red hair, although it was a shade lighter, and her long eyelashes curled on her cheeks as she slept.

She would lay down her life for her child, Jenna accepted resolutely. She would do everything in her power to protect and care for Maisie, and if that meant dealing with Alex Morrell on a daily basis, she had better get used to the idea.

Her shoulder was throbbing, and she toyed with the idea of taking one of the painkillers Alex's doctor had given her but decided against it. She hated taking pills, especially ones that might make her drowsy. Despite Alex's orders, she was determined to go to work the next day—and arrive on time.

Chris had gone to bed early, tired from travelling, and she was just about to do the same when the phone rang. She frowned as she went to answer it, recalling the spate of nuisance calls she had received a few months before. If Lee was starting his mind games again she would report the calls to the phone company, she vowed. But the voice at the other end of the line was very definitely not her exhusband's.

'Alex!' She fought to control the sudden pounding of her heart, and her voice sounded annoyingly breathless and excited.

'I thought I'd better phone and check that you're all right,' he told her, his own voice so cool that the little flame of pleasure in her breast was quickly doused. He was merely doing his duty, she reminded himself. It wasn't as if he actually cared about the injury she had received at the hands of the mugger. 'Have you taken the painkillers Guy prescribed?'

'I was just about to.'

'Hmm.' He was plainly disbelieving. 'Make sure you

do. What did Chris say about your attempt to be Superwoman?'

Jenna frowned. 'I haven't told him about it yet.'

'You haven't told your husband that you were injured?'

'It's nothing,' Jenna said quickly, belatedly remembering that he believed Chris to be her husband. She wasn't used to lying, and already it seemed that her one small lie was sprouting shoots like fast-growing ivy. If she wasn't careful she could very easily trip up. 'Thank you for ringing,' she murmured huskily, and heard him sigh.

'I owe you an apology; I should have believed the reason for your lateness this morning. I'm sorry.'

How could the sound of his voice affect her so strongly? Jenna thought frantically. Her legs felt like jelly, and a curious warmth, which had begun in the pit of her stomach, was flooding through her veins so that she felt hot and flustered. 'It's fine, really—a simple misunderstanding.' She hesitated, remembering the other misunderstanding that had occurred in the park, when he'd thought she was inviting him to kiss her, and she prayed that he was not experiencing the same flashback. 'I must go,' she mumbled. 'It's been a traumatic day.'

'For you and me both,' he replied, somewhat obliquely, but before she could decipher his meaning he bade her goodnight and hung up.

Chris offered to take Maisie to nursery the next morning, so that Jenna could catch an earlier train, and consequently she was the first to arrive at the office—although to her chagrin Alex was not there to witness it.

'Alex will be in court for most of the day,' Margaret explained. 'But he won't be happy when he discovers that you disobeyed him and came into work this morning.'

It was a pity Alex hadn't informed his numerous girlfriends that he would be out of the office, Jenna commented crabbily, after three different women had rung for him in the space of an hour.

'He is popular with the ladies,' Margaret agreed. 'But so far none of them have managed to pin him down. He's a brilliant barrister—a wonderful successor to his father— but I hope he meets someone special one day, otherwise work will take over his life.'

'Selina Carter-Lloyd seems very keen. Perhaps she's the one?' Jenna suggested. 'She was very insistent that I ask Alex to return her call.'

'Well, the two families have been friends for years, and Selina is very cultured and charming, but I don't believe Alex is in love with her.'

'What's love got to do with it?' Jenna muttered bleakly. She had been in love once, and look where it had got her. The husband from hell and a mortgage the size of third world debt. 'I'm not convinced that being in love is the best reason to get married.'

Margaret threw her a speculative glance, but said nothing. Her few gentle enquiries into Jenna's private life had been in vain and she didn't want to pry. If Jenna had problems she wished to confide she would do so in time, and Margaret was determined to provide a sympathetic ear. She had taken an instant liking to Jenna, and was certain that Pippa would not return to work after her maternity leave. She was also aware that Katrin Jefferstone would jump at the lower position if it meant working directly for Alex. Not if she could help it, Margaret vowed; sharing an office with Katrin was bad enough!

And with that thought in mind she invited Jenna to lunch.

Jenna had given up any hope of seeing Alex that day, and had almost convinced herself that it was a relief to be spared his sardonic humour. It was now four o'clock, she had worked like a Trojan all day, and was idly sketching a few ideas of illustrations for a children's book that she had written for Maisie when a voice in her ear made her jump.

'Very pretty—but it's not exactly work, is it?'

'Alex! I didn't hear you come in.' He moved with the stealth of a panther, she thought irritably, mortified to have been caught slacking.

'That's obvious,' Alex replied dryly. 'Although it beats me why you're here at all. I specifically told you to take the day off to allow your shoulder time to recover.'

There was no warmth in his blue eyes, and Jenna gave up. It seemed that she could do nothing right in this man's eyes. He was the boss, she reminded herself, and he had every right to expect high standards from his staff. If only he had returned to the office an hour earlier, he would have found her hard at work.

'These are exceptionally good,' he commented, flicking through her pages of drawings and ignoring the hand that tried to snatch them from him. 'You're very talented. Did you ever study art?'

'I was studying for a degree at St Martins,' she admitted, referring to the famous London art college. 'My work was often criticised for being too finicky, but I love intricate drawings and sketching minute detail.'

'So you have a degree in art?'

'No, I wasn't able to finish. There were problems, and studying didn't fit in with married life…' She tailed to a halt, unable to explain that her unplanned pregnancy had put an end to her dreams of being an illustrator. It would have been possible for her to return to college after Maisie's birth, but Lee had been adamant that if she had spare time on her hands she should find a job.

Alex gave her an assessing look and then glanced back

at the sketches, curious to know what kind of a man she had married—one who didn't encourage her talent, obviously. 'That's a pity,' he said quietly. 'Perhaps you'll have an opportunity to complete your studies in the future?'

'Perhaps,' she agreed, aware that there was no chance. That part of her life was over, and the hopes and aspirations she had once held seemed like childish dreams compared to the reality of life as a single mother.

'I'm only here briefly.' Alex moved away from her desk and distanced himself from the soft grey eyes that tugged at his heart. There was sadness in those eyes, a hint of regret, and he wanted to ask if her husband had forced her to give up studying the subject she loved.

It was none of his business, he reminded himself. Jenna Deane was married, had committed herself to another man, and he would do well to ignore the flare of awareness that dilated her pupils whenever their eyes met.

'Margaret has filled me in on most things. Were there any other calls I should know about?'

Jenna flicked through her diary. 'Selina Carter-Lloyd, Victoria Patterson, Sara Mittford. Although Miss Carter-Lloyd was the most persistent. You're obviously a popular guy.'

Her sniff, the tilt of her small nose as she gave him a disdainful stare said it all, and a smile tugged the corners of his mouth. 'You know what they say about all work and no play!'

His smile was her downfall, Jenna acknowledged ruefully. When he smiled his stern features softened, and she couldn't drag her gaze from the sensual curve of his mouth. Her tongue unconsciously traced the outline of her lips. Suddenly the air was charged with a tension that was almost tangible. Alex's smile had faded, his eyes narrowed, and there was a curious stillness about him, reminding her of a hunter stalking its prey. It was just a look, he wasn't even standing close to her, yet her body burned. She could feel her nipples harden, and to her shame she was aware of a melting warmth between her thighs.

'Alex, we weren't expecting to see you again today.' If Katrin was aware of the fraught tension in the office she ignored it, but Jenna recoiled from the look of sheer dislike she received from the other woman.

'I only stopped by to collect a few papers.' The spell was shattered and Alex strolled into his own office, knowing that his excuse was pathetic. There was nothing so vital that he needed to work on it that evening, but it had been a long day, and he had searched for a reason to return to his office, furious with himself for his need to see Jenna again.

'Alex! This is a surprise. Is everything all right?'

Couldn't he even visit his own office without everyone questioning his motives? Alex reined in his irritation and smiled at Margaret. 'Everything's fine, I just forgot a couple of things.'

'Right.' Margaret could not conceal her bafflement. Alex had an almost clinically precise mind, he never forgot anything, but as Jenna entered the office Margaret caught the unguarded look in his eyes and speculated on the reason for it.

'If there's nothing else, I'll be off now, Alex,' the younger woman murmured.

'Give me five minutes and I'll give you a lift.' Alex glanced up as Jenna hovered in the doorway. 'I've got a date this evening over your way.'

'There's really no need,' Jenna replied hastily, balking

at the idea of being alone with him for the forty-five minute journey across town.

'It's no problem.' His urbane smile disguised the determination in his voice.

To argue further would evoke Margaret's curiosity, so Jenna sighed. 'Thank you.'

There was no chauffeur-driven Bentley in the underground car park this time. Instead Alex led her over to an expensive-looking sports car and helped her into the passenger seat before coiling his long body behind the wheel. In the confines of the small car Jenna was achingly aware of his every movement, the way his hand brushed against her thigh every time he changed gear, and she squeezed as far as possible into the furthest corner of her seat.

'You can relax,' he said dryly, his patience paper-thin. 'I'm not in the habit of making a pass at unsuspecting secretaries while I'm driving.'

'I didn't think you were,' she snapped, her cheeks scarlet as she forced herself to sit properly and stare resolutely out of the window for the remainder of the journey.

Now she must appear rude and ungrateful, she thought miserably, searching for something to say to break the silence.

'Does Miss Carter-Lloyd—?'

'Where does Chris—?' Alex broke off and laughed. 'You first.'

'I just wondered if Miss Carter-Lloyd lived near here. You said you had a date,' Jenna reminded him.

'So I did. But, no, Selina doesn't live in this part of London.'

Which must mean he had a date with someone else, Jenna surmised, and wondered why she was glad that he did not date Selina Carter-Lloyd exclusively. 'What were you going to say?'

'I was going to ask what line of business Chris is in.'

'Chris is…um…' There was a frantic pause while she racked her brains. By Chris, he meant, of course, her husband. Her ex-husband was a fireman, but she had no desire to discuss Lee's heroics. Chris had mentioned that he was going to apply for a job at a popular fast food restaurant, so she murmured, 'He's a chef.'

'Really? Does he have any Michelin stars?'

'No, he works in a burger bar.'

Alex's brows shot upwards. 'So you're the main wage earner? Is that why you were unable to finish art college?'

'Kind of,' Jenna said, her tone non-committal. The conversation was getting way to personal, and she gave a sigh of relief as Alex turned into her road. 'Have a good evening,' she urged as she bade him goodnight.

'I intend to,' he replied, and she watched his car race off, deriding her over-active imagination at the thought of him with some stunningly beautiful girlfriend. Alex Morrell was out of her league, she reminded herself sternly, and she had the responsibility of a child to consider—a child he knew nothing about.

The rest of the week flew by, and despite the heavy workload Jenna found that she enjoyed the challenge of her job. It felt good to stretch her brain and realise that motherhood hadn't turned it completely to mush.

She enjoyed working for Alex Morrell—although enjoyed wasn't quite the right word. By turn he teased and terrified her, and she quickly came to respect his brilliant wit. She'd discovered that the only way she could work with him was to avoid looking directly at him. One glance at his hard, handsome face was enough to distract her mind from even the simplest task, and so she carefully studied the carpet, the desk or a point behind his shoulder whenever he addressed her. Occasionally, when her eyes sought him of their own accord, she found him watching her, but she dared not meet his gaze, her cheeks glowing pink as she hastily turned away.

With the notable exception of Katrin Jefferstone, the other staff were friendly and welcoming, and Jenna was touched when she was issued an invitation to the other senior partner's birthday dinner.

'Alex has made a private booking at the restaurant, and we're all meeting there straight from work,' Margaret explained. 'It's fairly informal, so I'm just going to bring another blouse to change into before we go.'

It seemed good advice, particularly as she had little else apart from her work suit that was suitable for an evening out, Jenna conceded. She had arranged for Maisie to spend the night with her neighbours, Nora and Charlie, and as she slipped into the cloakroom on Friday evening to change her top she found herself looking forward to the party.

She rarely went out these days—in fact since Maisie had been born her social life had dwindled to virtually nothing, and her bitter experience with Lee had put her off dating for good. After the few times when she had gone to dinner with one of the younger partners at her previous job, the disturbing phone calls had started. Lee had made them; she was certain of it. Despite sleeping with every woman he'd met between the ages of sixteen and sixty, he had a fiercely possessive streak. But she had never discovered how he was able to keep such close tabs on her movements, and it had been easier to give up socialising for good.

Everyone had assembled at the trendy wine bar that adjoined the restaurant, and Jenna blinked in surprise at some of the rather alarming African artwork on display, while heavy rock music pumped through the room.

'Charles is panicking at the thought of reaching fifty and is trying to recapture his youth,' Margaret confided with a chuckle. 'This sort of place is more your cup of tea than mine, but the food's supposed to be good, and there's music after dinner.'

Jenna ordered an orange juice, determined to keep a clear head. She felt awkward and out of place amidst the other staff, who were obviously all old friends. It was like being the new girl in the playground, she thought wryly, glancing round for Margaret, who seemed to have disappeared.

'Good evening, Jenna, is everything all right? You seem to be looking for someone.' Alex suddenly materialised at her side, and she swallowed nervously and addressed his tie.

'I was just wondering where Margaret had got to.'

'She's over there, talking to Charles's wife. Can I get you another drink?'

He moved forward to place his order and she found herself trapped between the bar and his chest, her senses immediately soaring into overdrive as she caught the subtle musk of his cologne.

'White wine, please,' she requested, hoping that the kick of alcohol would loosen her tongue, which suddenly seemed to be tied in knots.

'Nice carpet?' Alex enquired dryly, and she stared at him in confusion.

'What?'

'You seem to have a fascination with carpets; you certainly spend enough time studying them. Do you have a problem with looking at me, Jenna?'

'No! Of course not. Don't be ridiculous.'

Jenna felt her cheeks burn, unable to reveal that the sight of him did strange things to her equilibrium. His suit was designer, the exquisite cut of the jacket emphasising the width of his shoulders, and her fingers ached to stroke the fine white silk of his shirt. Anxious to deny his taunts, she stared at his face and felt a peculiar little dart of pain in her chest as she absorbed the masculine beauty of his bone structure. He was devastating, and, from the flirtatious glances that were bouncing his way, she wasn't the only woman to find him so.

'You could hardly be described as ugly, Alex; most of the women in this room are positively drooling at the sight of you.'

'But not you?' he queried lightly, and she shrugged.

'Is drooling a necessary requirement from your staff? If so then I will by all means. But may I point out that I am married?'

'There's no need to remind me,' he said curtly, and to her relief they were called in to dinner.

On her way into the restaurant Jenna slipped into the ladies' room, needing an excuse to delay her so that she could avoid sitting at the same table as Alex.

The glass of wine seemed to have gone straight to her head. She felt dizzy, and her cheeks were flushed, although whether that was a result of the alcohol or her close encounter with Alex she couldn't be sure. She stared despairingly at her reflection, noting her over-bright eyes. Her dilated pupils gave some clue to the heady excitement that filled her. She had to get over this ridiculous crush, she told herself sternly. It was so uncool to get in a flap every time she came within a five-mile radius of Alex, and if she wasn't careful others would notice—particularly him.

She had left her hair loose for the evening, and it swung

around her shoulders, making her look softer and sexier. For a moment she was tempted to scrape it back into a no-nonsense bun, but there was no time. The last thing she wanted to do was arrive at the table so late that she drew attention to herself. Hastily she adjusted the black jersey halter-neck top she had changed into before she left work, and groaned as she saw how lovingly it moulded her curves and emphasised the hard peaks of her nipples.

Wonderful, she thought grimly. She would either have to wear her jacket all through dinner and boil, or sit with her arms folded across her chest. Because no way was she going to flaunt the shaming evidence that Alex turned her on.

Fortunately Alex was seated at another table when she took her place next to Margaret, and she gave a sigh of relief that she could at least eat her dinner without feeling painfully self-conscious. With some distance between them she was able to covertly study him, her eyes feasting on the way his hard features softened when he smiled. The party was in Charles Metcalf's honour, yet it was Alex who held centre stage. He sat like a king surrounded by his courtiers, all eyes focused on him, while Katrin Jefferstone sat beside him, trying very hard—too hard— to act as his consort.

It was at that moment that Jenna realised she was not the only person suffering from an outsized case of hero-worship. A glance around the restaurant revealed that most women, even those with their partners, were affected by Alex's looks and sheer charisma. He must surely be aware of the looks directed at him—indeed, he probably felt as if he was sitting in a force nine gale with the amount of eyelash-batting taking place around him—and Katrin was certainly conscious of his popularity.

Katrin was a curious woman, nicknamed rather un-

kindly by some as the Ice Queen. She was cool to the
point of rudeness, kept herself very much to herself, and
seemed to have taken an instant dislike to Jenna.
Watching them, Jenna noted the edge of desperation in
the other woman's body language as she strove to keep
Alex's attention. They were subtle gestures—a toss of her
hair as she moved her head closer to his, her fingers resting lightly on his arm whenever he turned away—but they
added up to a woman who could barely contain her hunger. Katrin was in love with Alex. She too must be beset
by the same aching awareness that consumed Jenna whenever she was in Alex's company, but, unlike Jenna, she
made little effort to disguise the invitation in her eyes.

She was just one of the crowd, Jenna accepted bleakly.
Alex was a stunningly virile man, and she was no different
from the countless other women who prayed for him to
look their way. He looked up then, his eyes focusing directly on her, and she blushed at the ignominy of having
been caught studying him. Hastily she looked away, but
her eyes were drawn to his by a magnetic force and she
discovered that he was watching her, his expression unfathomable, although even across the width of the room
his personality swamped her.

'I think my husband is determined to dance with every
pretty girl in the restaurant.' An amused-sounding voice
interrupted her thoughts, and Jenna smiled at Charles
Metcalf's wife. 'It is his birthday, so I suppose I'll forgive
him. Charles, do mind Jenna's toes—she's only little.'

As the evening continued Jenna grew breathless and
pink-cheeked from her exertions on the dance floor, but
found she was thoroughly enjoying herself. Charles and
the other staff proved to be great company, and as she
was coerced into jiving to an old Elvis classic, she realised

how good it felt to throw off her responsibilities for a few hours.

'You appear to be having a good time. Dancing is obviously one of your hidden talents.'

She stumbled to a halt on the way back to her table, her path blocked by Alex's formidable chest. 'It's a wonderful party,' she agreed huskily, her heart performing its familiar somersault at the sight of him. 'I'd forgotten how much I love dancing.'

Her enjoyment had been evident; he had spent much of the evening watching her on the dance floor, unable to tear his eyes from her slender, graceful figure. Her hair gleamed like burnished gold on her pale shoulders, which were left bare by her halter-neck top. For a brief moment he envisaged winding his fingers into a silken strand, untying the ribbon that secured the top around her neck and drawing the material down to expose her breasts.

Jenna Deane was proving to be a distraction he could do without, he thought, and smiled derisively. Who was he kidding? Jenna was fast becoming an obsession he could do without. She was married, for God's sake! At the end of the evening she would go home to her husband. Another man had the right to fantasise about her delectable body, but not him.

'You're such an expert—you'd better give me a few lessons,' he suggested lightly. It would look odd if he didn't dance with his secretary, and the upbeat tempo of the music meant that there was little danger of body contact.

She could hardly refuse him, Jenna conceded, trying to mask her reluctance as she took his hand. She could manage one dance without making a fool of herself, surely? With one hand resting lightly on her waist, Alex danced as he did everything else—superbly. The music changed seamlessly from disco to a slow ballad, and Jenna stepped back, but his arm tightened imperceptibly around her waist, drawing her up close against him.

It was heaven and hell, and she moved in time with the music, trying her best to ignore the hardness of his thighs pressing on hers. She was so aware of him it hurt, every nerve-ending seemed ultra-sensitive, her senses heightened to such a degree that she was intoxicated by the sensual musk of his aftershave, and another, more subtle scent that was him. She focused rigidly on a point above his shoulder, and a frisson of excitement shot through her when he coiled a strand of her hair around his finger, his head bent so low that if she turned she would graze her cheek against his jaw.

The song eventually came to an end and she pulled abruptly out of his arms. 'I really must go before I miss the last train.'

'You can't possibly be planning to travel alone on the underground at this time of night?'

The impatient edge to his tone made her bristle. 'Why ever not? I live in a suburb of North London, not the Bronx. I'm quite capable of taking care of myself, Alex.'

His scathing look said it all. 'I take it your husband didn't offer to collect you and escort you safely home?'

'Chris is away this weekend, visiting friends.' That much was true anyway; her brother had travelled up to Nottingham to visit an old schoolfriend at the university.

'I'll take you home,' he said, in a tone that brooked no argument. But she argued anyway.

'Absolutely not. There's no need for you to leave the party on my behalf; honestly, Alex,' she added, a note of panic entering her voice, 'I'll be perfectly all right.'

He won, of course; there was really no contest. When Alex was determined to have his own way he was like a bulldozer, flattening any opposition, and Jenna was faced with causing a scene in front of the entire workforce or acceding to his will.

She remained silent on the journey home. Polite chit-chat was beyond her, and the simmering tension that hovered like a spectre between them stretched her nerves to screaming point.

'Do you have any plans while Chris is away?' His voice cut through the silence and she shrugged.

'I'll probably just rent a film and order a pizza.' She could hardly explain that she intended to spend her leisure time catching up on the chores that had built up all week, or that the highlight of the weekend would be cleaning out Maisie's pet rabbit.

She was filled with a sudden restlessness and wished that her life sounded more exciting. She loved spending time with Maisie, so why suddenly was it not enough? Why was she filled with a longing for adult company, and, if she was honest, for this particular man's company?

Alex caught the note of misery in her voice and wondered again about her husband. Would she spend the weekend missing him, impatiently waiting for him to return? He stared at her, his bland expression belying the surge of jealousy he felt as he imagined her eagerly welcoming the man he had briefly glimpsed when he had driven her home on her first day.

Maybe they would go to bed early on Sunday night. Doubtless they would make love. Jenna was a beautiful, sensual woman; she wasn't going to play Monopoly! He fought to blank out the stark image of her naked, pale limbs entwined with those of the man he had seen—her husband. This had to stop, he told himself furiously. Fantasising about his married secretary was repugnant, and he was sickened with himself. He had definitely been too long without a lover, but this weekend he could count on the companionship of a particularly charming ex-girlfriend, with whom he still enjoyed an open relationship. It was time he banished Jenna Deane well and truly from his mind, and the form of physical exercise he was planning for the next few nights should do the trick.

'How about you? Do you have anything exciting planned for the weekend?' Jenna queried, and his mouth curved into a sensual smile.

'I'm going to spend a few days at my apartment in Cannes.'

'Oh, yes, I'd forgotten.' She had a vivid image of him cavorting in Cannes with a gorgeous blonde and felt sick. Suddenly the interior of the car seemed claustrophobic; she urgently needed air and she fumbled to release her seat belt.

'Wait—the strap of your bag is tangled round the belt catch. What's the sudden hurry?'

She couldn't restrain the tremor that shook her as his hand closed around her wrist, and she shook her head frantically, her hair dancing wildly on her shoulders. 'Nothing, I need to…'

He was close, so close that even in the dim interior of the car she could see the laughter lines at the corner of his eyes and the grooves on either side of his mouth. His face was suddenly a taut mask.

'No, I need…to do this,' he muttered, his voice so deep she could barely make out the words. But she was in no doubt of his intent. His fingers tightened on her arm while his other hand cupped her jaw and exerted gentle pressure so she tilted her face up to his. His lips moved as soft as a butterfly over hers, caressed briefly and then lifted and paused fractionally before skimming again, his touch as light as gossamer.

Jenna shuddered and closed her eyes, not wanting to see the contempt in his when he realised that she had been lost from the moment he'd first touched her. She waited in trepidation for him to release her with a disparaging comment, and her heart leapt when, instead, his lips brushed over hers once more, the pressure stronger this time, stirring her response.

Her lips parted. She couldn't have stopped her response even if she had wanted. Her mind and body were at war and her body was the runaway victor. The tentative slide of her tongue was the tinder that set the fire ablaze, and he groaned low in his throat as sanity succumbed to the flames of a passion that had been building inexorably all week. His hand slid the length of her jaw to cup her nape, forcing her head up so that he could take her mouth in a devastating assault that racked her, his tongue probing between her lips, demanding entry and forcing her to accept a level of eroticism that was beyond anything she had ever known.

When at last he lifted his head he stared down at her, his eyes glittering like twin sapphires, but there was no warmth in their depths and Jenna shivered, suddenly feeling chilled to the bone.

'Chris is a fool. If you were my wife I wouldn't trust to leave you alone for a day, let alone an entire weekend.'

His words were like a slap in the face, and she flung open the car door, desperate to get away from him. 'Save the sympathy for my husband, Alex. The only fool is me. I knew I should have caught the train. I would have been far safer travelling alone on the underground than accepting a lift from you.'

She had turned her key in the lock and opened the front door before she heard his car furiously roar away, and in the recesses of her mind she appreciated the degree of care for her well-being that had made him wait until she was safely inside.

She was too wound up to sleep and paced the house, reliving the moments in his arms and haranguing herself for her pathetic weakness where Alex Morrell was concerned. Why had he kissed her? Had she made her fascination for him so obvious that he'd decided to take advantage of the fact that her husband was away, sure that she would be a willing partner for the night? He might be spoilt for choice of female company, but what man would turn down a one-night stand with a woman whose married status, he believed, would mean she would make no further demands on him?

It was almost one in the morning when she forced herself to get ready for bed. In a few hours Maisie would be home, and she needed to be bright and happy for her daughter. She had responsibilities, a child to bring up without the support of a father, and there was no place in her life or bed for Alex.

As she doused the bedside lamp the phone rang, its strident sound making her jump, and she fumbled in the dark to answer it.

'Alex?' She could think of no one else who would ring her at that hour, but the silence on the line filled her with dread, and the hoarse breathing, which in the light of day she could have mocked, sounded ominously threatening. 'Go to hell, you sick idiot,' she yelled, before she slammed down the receiver and burst into tears.

CHAPTER FOUR

JENNA returned to work on Monday morning, safe in the knowledge that Alex was in France and she was spared having to face him for a couple of days. She had spent the weekend tearing herself to shreds over the way she had responded to his kiss, and was dreading seeing him again, certain that she would be subjected to his particular brand of cruel sarcasm.

The day dragged, and by five o'clock she was forced to admit that she missed him. Even worse, she was counting the hours until he returned—which must make her some sort of masochist, she thought despairingly.

'Alex has just called to say he won't be coming back this week,' Margaret announced. 'Apparently the weather on the Riviera is wonderful. Although, between you and me, I think he's met up with an old girlfriend. He sounded...' Margaret gave a conspiratorial chuckle '...tired, but the break will do him good. I'll just have to reschedule his diary.'

Good for him, Jenna thought as she trudged through the rain to the station, trying to ignore the sick jealousy that burned in the pit of her stomach. It was none of her business what he got up to, she reminded herself. He could be enjoying himself with the entire French ladies' rugby team for all she cared, and at least while he was away she didn't have to worry about him breathing down her neck. Alex was an attractive, virile man; of course he had lovers—dozens of them, probably, and, just like Lee, he was doubtless unable to remain faithful to any of them.

On Friday morning she raced into the office, fifteen minutes late and cursing public transport, and collided with a familiar figure, her heartbeat accelerating as she found herself in Alex's arms.

'I thought you were supposed to be living it up in Cannes?' she accused, frantically trying to disguise the flare of pleasure in her eyes.

'Is that why you're late? You didn't feel the same urgency to arrive on time, believing that I was still away?' He watched the way she hastily disentangled herself from him through hooded lids, and inhaled sharply as he caught the drift of her perfume.

'That's grossly unfair; as you once pointed out, I have no control over the vagaries of London Transport.' She glared at him, hands on hips, her eyes flashing with the temper that was her only weapon against the insidious warmth that flooded through her at the sight of him.

'When you've calmed down, I'd like you to bring me the Robson file. Margaret has some letters for you to type—oh, and we're flying to Paris on Monday. I assume your passport is in order?'

'Paris!' She stared at him in consternation. 'For how long?'

'A couple of days.' He noted the panic in her eyes and sighed irritably. 'It's not Mars, Jenna, it's just across the Channel. Do you have a problem?'

'Absolutely not,' she lied as she followed him into his office, her mind already reeling with preparations.

It was the first time she had been asked to travel with him. Up until now her job had worked out better than she had anticipated, and she had been home at six each evening, just after Nora had collected Maisie from the day nursery. It was only a couple of days, she reassured herself. Maisie would be perfectly happy staying with Nora and Charlie, and Chris would be on hand to help out. She mentally listed all the tasks that needed to be done before she went away. She would have to reschedule taking the cat to the vet, and fit in an evening dash to the supermarket before she left. Alex's words went straight over her head.

'Sorry, what was that?' she murmured into the taut silence that spoke volumes about his annoyance at being ignored.

'I said there's no need to come into work on Monday; I'll pick you up from home. You'll need to travel in something comfortable, but pack an evening dress as we'll be dining with my client.'

Would her faithful black skirt and a blouse constitute evening dress? Jenna wondered as her mind made the short trip through her wardrobe. It would have to do. Maisie needed a new winter coat, and the boiler was on the blink; she certainly couldn't afford to buy a new outfit.

'One other thing.' His voice halted her as she was about to escape to her own office. 'Do something with that suit.'

'Do what with it?' she queried with a puzzled frown.

'Bin it, preferably.'

'It's the only smart suit I own.'

'So I gathered,' Alex replied dryly, and she flushed at his implied criticism of her appearance.

Admittedly she had worn her grey suit to the office every day, but she had bought a couple of new blouses and taken time with her hair and make-up. She didn't look that much of a mess, surely?

'Perhaps you can sweet-talk your husband into splashing out? A few good-quality outfits are a necessary requirement of your job.'

'Alex, by the time I've repaid my mortgage I'll be ninety-seven. I can't afford a new wardrobe of clothes. If you want me to go to Paris, it's in this or nothing.' She stalked out of his office, bristling with indignation and humiliation.

His dulcet comment followed her. 'Nothing could prove interesting.' But it failed to evoke even a ghost of a smile.

It was the morning from hell, she decided later, having discovered that she had deleted an hour's work from her computer by mistake. Alex's presence unsettled her, she felt on edge whenever he was near, and she had managed to spill an entire cup of coffee over his desk simply because her fingers felt as though they had turned into bananas.

'I'm sorry,' she had muttered, close to tears as she attempted to blot the pile of coffee-stained documents in front of him.

'Don't worry about it.' His unexpected kindness had been worse than if he'd lost his temper. She'd almost wished he would crucify her with one of his scathing comments, because at least then she could have kidded herself that she hated him.

'I think I'd better buy you lunch. That way you might actually get some work done this afternoon.'

He materialised in front of her desk and her gaze focused on his chest, admiring the way his blue silk shirt echoed the colour of his eyes. He looked so gorgeous it hurt: tanned and fit, the superb cut of his charcoal-coloured suit emphasising his height and the formidable width of his shoulders.

'I've got a sandwich in my bag—cheese and pickle,' she added, before he could find fault with her lunch.

'It wasn't a request, Jenna, it was an order. So save your breath and let's go.'

She grudgingly had to admit that she felt better after a plate of lasagne, and at his request filled him in on the week's events, knowing that he would accuse her of sulking if she did not.

After lunch he steered her into a department store, and she frowned as he led the way to the designer ladieswear section. If he intended to ask her opinion on titillating lingerie for his girlfriend he would find himself sporting a pair of silk cami-knickers on his head!

'My companion would like to see a selection of formal daywear, and she also needs a couple of evening dresses,' Alex explained to the assistant, and Jenna glanced over her shoulder, looking for the said companion.

'We'll need to look at the petite section,' the assistant said, smiling at Jenna, and realisation suddenly dawned.

'They'll never fit you,' she snapped at Alex furiously. 'And no way on this earth will I allow you to buy my clothes.'

'I had a feeling you'd say that. The trouble with you, Jenna, is that you're so predictable. Now, there's an easy way of doing this or a hard way. The easy way is for you to go with the assistant and choose a suit and something for the evening. The hard way entails me coming into the changing rooms with you.'

His eyes flashed with steely determination, and, mindful that they were causing a scene, Jenna could only glare at him.

'You're my boss, Alex, not God himself,' she hissed.

'Same thing,' he told her urbanely. 'At least as far as you're concerned. I'll be back in an hour,' he informed the assistant, who visibly wilted under the full charm of his smile, and then he was gone, leaving a stunned silence in his wake.

The assistant did her best, but Jenna could only be coerced into choosing a soft ecru-coloured suit and one black evening dress—which, she had to admit, was to die for. Even then she found that she needed shoes, handbag and a black beaded purse to match the dress, and when Alex returned she was frantically trying to tot up the cost in her head.

'Stop fretting,' he told her bluntly. 'Think of the clothes as part of your uniform. Many companies provide their staff with suitable work clothes, and if it really bothers you so much, consider them on loan from Morrell and Partners. You can hand them back at the end of your contract.'

He handed over his credit card to the sales assistant and Jenna paled as the total flashed up on the till. She would repay him every penny, she vowed. It might stretch her overdraft to the limit, but she would not be beholden to Alex Morrell.

They walked back to the office in silence, Alex seemingly lost in his thoughts, but as the lift whisked them up to the top floor he turned to Jenna. 'Will the clothes cause a problem with Chris?'

'I doubt he'll even notice them,' she replied honestly, forgetting for a moment that he thought Chris was her husband.

There was something strange about her marriage, Alex decided. He had tried to ignore the gossip circulating round the office that Jenna's marriage was an unhappy one, and the fact that she pointedly avoided talking about Chris. If nothing else her husband must be blind, he thought grimly. She was achingly beautiful, even when angry, he thought with a wry smile. Right now she was positively bristling with outrage at his heavy-handedness, but it was better that she was furious with him than embarrassed by her lack of suitable clothes when they dined with the elite of Parisian society.

'Miss Carter-Lloyd is here to see you,' Margaret announced on their return, and Alex stifled a groan. A dose of Selina he could do without.

'If the lovely Selina has her way, Alex will be tied up for the rest of the day,' Margaret whispered to Jenna, as Alex closed the interconnecting door between the offices. 'Not literally, of course—although knowing Selina anything's possible. I don't suppose she was very happy when he took off to Cannes without her.'

'Pity he didn't stay there,' Jenna muttered, and Margaret threw her a curious glance.

'I thought he was going straight from Cannes to Paris to see his client, and I had the shock of my life when he walked out of his office first thing this morning,' she confided. 'I wonder why he came back.'

Jenna didn't know, and certainly didn't care. Tucked away at the bottom of one the carrier bags, beneath her new dress, she had discovered a set of exquisite underwear, its sheer black silk blatantly sexy. A new suit for work was one thing, and the black evening dress was pushing it, but she drew the line at underwear.

'You appear to have left something of yours in with my shopping,' she began, brandishing the underwear in front of her as she marched into Alex's office, and came to an abrupt halt when she found him locked in a passionate embrace with a statuesque blonde. 'Oh, I'm sorry.'

It was ridiculous to feel so utterly betrayed, she reasoned, but nothing, not even Lee's brazen infidelity, had prepared her for the pain of seeing Alex kiss another woman. He meant nothing to her, she told herself frantically, but the knife in her chest cut deep, and something of her despair must have shown in her eyes, causing Alex's gaze to narrow as he pulled out of his companion's arms.

'Can't you see we're busy?' the woman snapped, looking down at Jenna with haughty dismissal.

'I'm sorry. I didn't realise…' Jenna backed towards the door, shoving the silk underwear behind her, but Alex's cool tones stopped her.

'Now that you're here, I'd like to introduce you to Selina Carter-Lloyd. Selina, this is my temporary secretarial assistant, Jenna Deane.'

Selina gave a brief, uninterested nod and turned her back on Jenna, wrapping her arms around Alex's neck like a limpet of Amazonian proportions.

She had to be six feet tall, Jenna decided, noting the way Selina's face was almost on a level with Alex's. She was well built and broad-shouldered, strikingly attractive rather than beautiful, with thick honey-blonde hair and the careless elegance of someone who had grown up with money.

'Why can't you come to Hampshire for the weekend?' she pouted. 'You know you have an open invitation to stay at Amberley. Mummy was saying only yesterday that you haven't visited for ages.'

'Your parents are very kind, and I'll get down as soon as I can. But I'm going to be tied up with work all weekend, before I fly to Paris on Monday.'

'You know what they say about all work and no play,' Selina murmured. 'You need a wife, Alex, someone who can persuade you to relax more.'

There was no doubting the form of persuasion Selina had in mind, Jenna thought disparagingly. The woman had the subtlety of a carthorse, but Alex didn't seem to mind. Perhaps marriage was on his agenda after all, and Selina, the daughter of a judge, would make him an eminently suitable wife.

The thought left a hollow feeling around her heart, and

she stared at him bleakly when he came back into the office, having escorted Selina to the door with the promise that he would call her.

'In future, knock before you barge into my office,' he bit out furiously, and her temper flared.

'I said I was sorry, but I didn't realise you were… entertaining.'

'I could have been cavorting on my desk stark naked if I'd so desired.'

Jenna's breath snagged in her throat as she pictured his gloriously bare body, the image so starkly erotic that she couldn't bring herself to meet his gaze.

'And I wasn't "entertaining", as you so delicately put it, I merely gave Selina a friendly kiss.'

'I thought you were eating her,' Jenna returned haughtily, and despite himself Alex's lips twitched.

No one ever answered him back. Even Margaret, who had worked for him for years, used subtle persuasion to influence his decisions, but Jenna suffered no such inhibitions. She gave as good as she received, and he found himself admiring her for her nerve.

Somehow this tiny, feisty redhead had crept under his skin, and, rather like an irritating rash, he couldn't seem to get rid of her. She was staring at him now, with those enormous Bambi eyes, and as his gaze focused on the tremulous curve of her mouth, his smile faded. He had dated many beautiful women over the years; he had never professed to be a monk. But the few days he had spent in Cannes had been akin to taking Holy Orders, notable only for his distinct lack of desire for Angelina or any other woman. His loss of libido had been frankly embarrassing, and he had used the excuse that he needed to return to the office as a way of ending an awkward situation, leaving behind a patently bemused Angelina.

Of course it would have made more sense to stop over in Paris on his way back from Cannes, and he refused to admit to himself or anyone else that he had only flown straight to London because he ached to see Jenna again. For some reason this woman had the ability to distract his usually disciplined thought process, even whilst he was in court, and at night she haunted his dreams, featuring in erotic fantasies that were totally inappropriate when dawn heralded the reality that she was married to another man.

Perhaps that was the key to her allure—the reason for his fascination with her, he surmised grimly. He had been blessed, or cursed, with a fiercely competitive streak and a determination to win what he wanted from life. Did he want Jenna because she was beyond his reach? The thought hovered uncomfortably in his subconscious, and he turned away from her to stare blankly at his computer screen. Was he really contemplating breaking up her marriage simply to prove a point?

Jenna returned home that evening, already fretting about the Paris trip with Alex, but the letter waiting for her from her ex-husband's solicitors banished everything from her mind. The letter briefly reminded her that under the terms of her divorce Lee had been granted access visits to his daughter every other weekend, and that if she continued to prevent him from seeing Maisie the matter would have to go back to court.

'I've never tried to stop Lee. At first, when the divorce was finalised, I encouraged him to visit Maisie,' she explained to Chris. 'I wanted them to maintain a good relationship. But Lee was so unreliable, he either showed up late or not at all, and after a while I stopped phoning him to remind him that it was his weekend to visit. I don't understand what this is all about,' she muttered worriedly,

waving the letter in the air. 'Why didn't he just ring me
to say he wanted to renew contact with Maisie? Why involve the courts?'

'He's playing mind games with you,' Chris told her
sympathetically. 'He always was a manipulative bastard,
and behind his pretty-boy image he has a devious brain.'

'But why?' Jenna shook her head in frustration. 'As far
as I'm concerned there was never an argument over his
access to Maisie, but he's never taken much interest in
her. All he ever wanted was money, which is why I extended the mortgage on the house and paid him his share.
I can't help thinking that he's up to something.'

She tried to put the letter out of her mind, and an en-
ergetic trip to the park with Maisie on Saturday morning
helped put her worries into perspective, but her reprieve
was short-lived.

'Hello, Jenna, you're looking good.' Lee was lounging
against the bonnet of his car when she followed Maisie
and her little tricycle up the hill.

'Lee, this is a surprise.' She was determined to keep
calm, but already her hackles were rising under his cocky,
faintly insulting appraisal. 'I take it you're here to see
Maisie?'

'Course I am.' Lee hunkered down in front of the tricycle. 'Hello, Maisie, you got a kiss for your daddy?'

The little girl blinked solemnly at him, and then at
Jenna. 'Daddy?' she queried innocently, and Jenna
dredged up an encouraging smile.

'Daddy's come to visit you, darling. Isn't that nice?'
She glanced back at Lee, her expression cool. 'You can
hardly expect her to leap into your arms. It's been so long
since you bothered to visit she barely recognises you.'

'Then it's time I made it up to her,' Lee replied, plainly
unconcerned by her tangible antagonism. 'From now on

I'll be visiting every other weekend—maybe more often, if the courts agree. And I'll want to take her away with me. For the day at first, but as she gets older for the whole weekend.'

'There was no need to involve your solicitor. I've never stopped you from seeing Maisie,' Jenna pointed out, trying to keep the tremor out of her voice. 'What are you up to, Lee? You haven't bothered with Maisie since the day she was born. Why the sudden determination to be Super Dad?'

Lee ran a hand through his blond highlights, taking care not to ruffle the style, and gave a sly grin. 'I'm getting married again, and I want Maisie to have a proper, stable home life—not be constantly dumped with babysitters while you screw your boyfriend on the front seat of his bloody car.'

Jenna stared at him with a mixture of horror and disbelief. 'How on earth do you know—?' she began, and stopped abruptly. She was damned if she would explain herself to Lee.

'A little bird told me,' he said, tapping the side of his nose, his smile telling her that he was aware of her discomfort. 'There's not a lot you get up to that I don't know about, darling, and I'm not going to stand by and allow my little girl to be brought up by a succession of uncles—even ones who drive flash cars.'

Jenna was so shocked by Lee's visit that she seriously contemplated phoning Alex to tell him she could not accompany him to Paris. But what excuse could she give? she fretted, during a long, sleepless night. Alex had employed her in the belief that she had few commitments and would be constantly at his beck and call. She could hardly reveal that her personal life was growing more complicated by the minute without running the risk of losing her job, and if she were unemployed it would only serve to increase Lee's determination to win custody of Maisie. Common sense told her that Lee didn't stand a realistic chance of taking Maisie away from her, but he was clever, in a crafty, manipulative way, and although she hated to admit it she had always been secretly afraid of him.

The throaty roar of Alex's car could be heard long before he pulled up outside the house on Monday morning, and she snatched up her bags and ran down the front path.

She didn't know how Lee was able to keep track of her movements, and perhaps he had just said it to frighten her, but she was taking no chances. She didn't want him to find out that she had gone away without Maisie.

'What's the hurry?' Alex queried with a frown as she stumbled to a halt in front of him. 'You're not late.'

'I just thought you'd want to get away,' she muttered, casting a furtive glance along the street, as if expecting to see Lee spring out from behind a tree.

She glanced back at Alex and felt a hand close around her heart at the sight of him. He was handsome in a suit, but in black jeans and matching sweater he was stunning, his tan corduroy jacket adding a sexy informality to his appearance. At least in the office rules of convention deemed him remote, but now his casual clothes and relaxed air made him seem dangerously accessible, and to her chagrin she found that her legs had turned to jelly.

'In you get, then.' He opened the car door to allow her to scramble inside with more haste than dignity, and he frowned as he spied the haunting vulnerability in her eyes. 'Do you feel all right? You look very pale.'

'I'm fine.' She couldn't avoid his gaze when he cupped her chin and tilted her face, the gentle concern she could see mirrored in his blue eyes causing tears to burn behind her eyelids.

She looked achingly fragile, and Alex felt a curious pain in his chest as he noted the smudges beneath her eyes and the droop of her mouth.

'I'm just tired, that's all. I didn't get much sleep last night.'

'Spare me the details.' He released her chin abruptly, but as she turned away he caught sight of a purple bruise on her temple, noting the way she quickly shook her head so that her hair covered the mark. 'What have you done to your head? You're hurt.'

'It's nothing.' She shied away as he pushed her hair back. 'I walked into a door. I'm notoriously clumsy,' she added with a feeble laugh.

Hitting her head on the doorframe was the truth, but she couldn't reveal that Lee had stormed into the house and had knocked into her—deliberately, she was sure— and that she had cracked her head so hard she had literally seen stars. During her marriage Lee had never been deliberately violent, but he was spiteful, and she had suffered numerous accidents—like the time he had slammed a car door and broken two of her fingers.

Alex stared at her in silence, filled with a sudden surge of anger. The bruise on her forehead had not resulted from any accident, he was certain of it, and her tension, the way she avoided his gaze, only reinforced his suspicions.

'Is your husband annoyed about the trip? I could talk to him.'

'No! Leave it, Alex, please. There are a lot of things you don't understand.'

A heavy silence filled the car, and Alex had to force himself to keep within the speed limit until they reached the motorway, then he gunned the engine, exorcising his frustration with sheer speed.

'Why are we going to Paris?' Jenna asked, desperate to break the taut silence. For some reason Alex was furious, his pent-up aggression an almost tangible force, his jaw rigid, although the expression in his dark eyes gave nothing away. 'Maybe you should fill me in on a few details.'

'Sebastian Vaughn is an old friend,' he explained heavily. 'We were at university together, and at the moment he's staying in Paris with his French grandmother. It's Madame Roussel's eightieth birthday party tomorrow, and obviously Seb doesn't want to miss it, but I need to go over a few things with him before his case goes to court on Friday.

'Seb is married to Ellisa Trent, the famous model,' Alex continued. 'On the surface they appear to be the golden couple who have it all, but the reality is that they've spent the last five years trying to have a child. Ellisa has suffered numerous miscarriages, but this time her pregnancy was going well—until a photographer from the paparazzi chased her relentlessly, demanding an interview. In her desperation to escape she stumbled into the road and was hit by a car.'

Jenna gasped. 'Was she badly hurt?'

'At first it was feared she would lose the baby. Seb is a mild-mannered politician, a rising star of the opposition party renowned for his pacifist views, but faced with his wife's injuries, and possibly the loss of his child, he saw red. He attacked the photographer and smashed his camera, and now he faces charges of assault and criminal damage.'

'So you're defending him,' Jenna murmured. 'But presumably his actions were witnessed and the photographer will testify against him? It's a desperately sad story, but what defence can there be?'

'I need to prove that there were mitigating circumstances for his behaviour, which was completely out of character. If Seb gets a criminal record his political career will be over. Some sections of the media act with complete disregard for decency. Just because Seb and Ellisa are in the public eye, they're deemed a legitimate target for the tabloid press, and the law does little to protect their privacy.' There was a harsh edge to Alex's tone and Jenna shivered, glad that she would never have to face him in a court. He would make a formidable adversary.

'It's obviously a subject that's close to your heart,' she remarked, and he nodded.

'Fortunately Ellisa and the baby are okay, but I sympathise with Seb. He was only doing what any man would do—protecting the woman he loves.'

'Do I detect a streak of romanticism?' Jenna queried lightly, aware of a curious pain in her chest at the image Alex's fierce words evoked. How wonderful it must be to be loved and protected in the way he described. 'I would never have imagined it of you, Alex.'

Alex shrugged. 'Perhaps it is old-fashioned, in these days of equality between the sexes, but I would lay down my life if I had a wife and child to protect. I believe that marriage is a lifetime commitment,' he added quietly, 'especially when children are involved.'

'You don't think there are any valid reasons for divorce?' Jenna queried, struggling to disguise the bitterness in her voice.

She too had believed in the sanctity of marriage—and she had done her best, hadn't she? Had stuck with Lee when most women would have given up on him? But Lee had shared very different views from Alex's, and love had been an illusion quickly shattered. In the end she had been the one to demand an end to her marriage, but Lee had walked away without a second glance and had taken little interest in his daughter. His sudden decision to renew contact with Maisie had come out of the blue, and she was suspicious about his motives for getting in touch.

'Of course there are valid reasons for ending a marriage,' Alex murmured, throwing her a curious glance. 'And domestic violence must top the list.'

His fingers tightened round the steering wheel and he had to force himself to concentrate on the road ahead as he remembered the bruise on her forehead, the way she hung her head so that her hair swung across her face in an effort to hide the injury. She looked pale, her body as taut as an overstrung bow, and he wanted to pull into the nearest lay-by, stop the car and draw her into his arms. Something was seriously wrong with her marriage, he knew it instinctively, but he couldn't force her to confide in him.

She was watching him now, her eyes huge and wary, and he knew she would hate him if he voiced his suspicions that her husband had hit her. It was nothing to be ashamed of, damn it, but she was fiercely proud and would never forgive him for intruding on her private life. All he could do was bide his time and hope to win her trust—but that in itself was laughable when he couldn't look at her without wanting her.

The journey continued in silence, and Jenna stared unseeingly out of the window, lost in her thoughts, until Alex murmured, 'Here we are,' and she realised that they had turned off the main road and swung through the gates of a small private airfield.

'I assumed we would be flying from Gatwick,' she said in surprise. 'Where are we, exactly?'

'Elstree Aerodrome. I keep my plane here.'

'Your plane!' She didn't know what she had been expecting—a uniformed pilot and a private jet, possibly. Certainly not the small twin-engine Cessna that Alex pointed out. For a moment all her worries about Maisie and her ex-husband were forgotten. 'I'm not flying to France in that.'

'I'm a fully qualified private pilot.'

'I don't care if you're the Red Baron. I hate flying at the best of times, and that thing looks like an egg carton with wings.'

'Jenna!' It was amazing how much persuasive charm he could infuse into her name. His voice was as rich as clotted cream, the expression in his eyes warm and gently teasing as his bad mood evaporated. 'I thought you were a brave tigress, don't disappoint me now.'

'Why a tigress?' she stammered. Faced with his beguiling charm, she felt as daring as a jellyfish—and it had nothing to do with her fear of flying.

He shrugged his shoulders eloquently, seeming suddenly big and overpowering in a very small car. 'You don't seem to be afraid of anything. You stand up for yourself. You certainly give as good as you get with me.'

Was there a touch of admiration in his voice? He was a strong-willed man; perhaps he liked women who mirrored that strength? Suddenly she *was* a tigress. What was so different between a commercial jet and a light aircraft anyway? As long as it went up and stayed up!

'Okay, I'll give it a go,' she agreed, and was rewarded with a smile that took her breath away, the curve of his mouth a sensual invitation that she longed to accept.

'You're a star, gorgeous.' He was so relaxed, so different from the hard-faced barrister she had grown used to, and his throwaway compliment caused goosebumps to prickle her skin.

She stood by the plane and watched him complete his pre-flight checks. He was a man who was way out of her reach, and in his eyes she was a married woman. It was time she started to act like one.

'Why do you have to waggle the wings?' she queried nervously. 'Are they likely to fall off?'

'Of course not. Come on—in you get.' There was a high step into the plane and he simply lifted her off her feet and deposited her in the cabin. 'It'll be fun, trust me. If you get scared I promise I'll hold your hand.'

'Just keep your hands on the steering wheel, or whatever it is.' She glanced around the cockpit at the levers and dials and shuddered; the tigress was feeling as weak as a kitten!

It was claustrophobic in the small cockpit, and Jenna couldn't quell her feelings of panic as Alex handed her a headset and taxied the plane to the runway. Trust me, he had urged, and she found that she did so utterly. There was an air of strength about him, of dependability, and she was sure he would pilot the plane with the same level of expertise that he did everything else, but even so she screwed her eyes shut as they rose into the air.

'That wasn't so bad, was it? You can look now.' His hand curled around both of hers, offering moral support, but the clasp of his strong fingers burned her skin and did nothing to steady her racing heart.

Cautiously she peeped from beneath her lashes to see the fields and trees spread like a colourful patchwork of autumn hues, the houses already the size of a model village. It was a beautiful day, the sky a cloudless blue, and she let out a shaky breath and gradually relaxed.

'Want to take the controls?'

'Absolutely not!'

Her eyes were like saucers and he grinned and squeezed her hand. 'It's really not difficult. Maybe I'll do a couple of loops.'

'Don't you dare! Alex, promise me. I just want to go in a straight line. No clever stuff.'

She could become seriously addicted to the sound of his laughter, the way his eyes crinkled at the edges and his mouth curved, she thought as her heart lurched in her chest. She could become seriously addicted to him. And with a determined effort she wriggled her hands from his grasp and concentrated on the scenery below.

CHAPTER FIVE

PARIS was everything Jenna had imagined: elegant, exciting—and romantic, she added to her list with a groan of despair. Paris was a city for lovers. Everywhere she'd looked during her brief sightseeing trips with Alex there had been couples wandering hand in hand, young·lovers kissing with unrestrained passion in the shadow of the Eiffel Tower.

She was always glad to return to the hotel, where their meetings with Sebastian Vaughn had provided a break in the unspoken tension between her and Alex. Glad too that she had been bullied into buying her new clothes, she conceded. The hotel was an oasis of discreet grandeur that exuded wealth, and she shuddered to think of the pained glances she would have received had she worn her ill-fitting suit.

That evening, as she slipped into her black evening dress, ready for Sebastian's grandmother's party, her confidence rose by several notches. The dress was deceptively simple, but the exquisite cut of the material, the way it sheathed her body, more than warranted its exorbitant price tag. Despite its simplicity it was an overtly sexy dress, something she hadn't appreciated when she had tried it on, and for a moment she quailed at the way the neckline dipped to reveal a daring amount of cleavage, her breasts full and pale against the black silk.

Hearing her knock on the interconnecting door to his room, Alex took a deep breath before he swung away from the window and the night-time view of Paris.

'I'm ready—on time too. You did say seven.'

'So I did.' For a second he was unable to disguise the flare of hunger in his eyes, but almost instantly his lashes lowered and when he looked at Jenna again his expression was cool and aloof. 'You look charming, I like the dress.'

'Thank you,' Jenna murmured, instantly deflated.

What had she expected? she chided herself. She had wanted to wow him, the insidious voice in her head prompted. She had wanted him to find her gorgeous and irresistible, but instead he had shown no more than polite interest in his married secretary.

During this trip he had gone out of his way to be charming, determined to show her as much of Paris as possible in spite of spending a lot of time working on Sebastian Vaughn's defence case. He had been a witty and entertaining companion, friendly yet remote, and she had been aware of an unspoken tension that sizzled between them. On several occasions she had looked up to find him watching her with eyes as dark as midnight, but each time he had quickly averted his gaze, as if embarrassed that he had been caught out. She was not obtuse, no inexperienced virgin, and she recognised the heat of desire he was so determined to deny, and shared his hunger.

She was tempted to tell him the truth about Lee, but something held her back. To reveal that she was divorced would pave the way for what, exactly? An affair? Perhaps not even that. Perhaps just a one-night stand while they were swept away by the atmosphere of the world's most romantic city.

'Shall we go?' He sauntered across the room and proffered his arm with a nonchalant ease she could only admire, and the shiver that ran the length of her body had little to do with the cool night air.

In his black dinner jacket and white silk shirt he looked

devastatingly handsome—a fact that did not pass unnoticed by just about every woman in the room when they arrived at Madame Roussel's magnificent apartment. He would turn heads wherever he went, Jenna acknowledged bleakly. She was not the only woman to be turned on by his raw masculinity. But she hoped she hid her response a little better; several of the female guests were positively salivating.

'Alex, I'm so happy to see you again.' Sebastian's grandmother held out her hand and smiled as Alex lifted it to his lips. 'It is a grand occasion, do you think, my eightieth birthday?'

'You look magnificent, *madame*, I can hardly warrant the years.'

'And you are such a flirt.' Eyes as clear and bright as those of a woman half her age sparkled with pleasure, and Clotilde Roussel's welcoming smile encompassed Jenna. 'So, you are going to help my grandson, Alex? Do you think you can save him from the consequences of his momentary madness?'

'I'll do my best,' Alex assured her, but Madame Roussel's rather haughty expression crumpled.

'Sebastian is a good man, a gentleman in the true sense of the word. His only crime is that he adores his wife and wanted to protect her from the intrusions of the paparazzi. He was driven to desperate actions and now he stands to lose not just his career but also his good name. I know you will do everything in your power to help him, Alex. Ellisa is not with us tonight,' Madame Roussel continued. 'Seb refused to allow her to travel, with the baby due so soon, and I know he is impatient to get back to her, but this court case is looming and he is so worried. Perhaps you can persuade Sebastian to forget his problems for one night.'

It was an amazing party, Jenna thought as she glanced around the packed room, almost blinded by the array of diamonds on display. The cream of Parisian society was present—the men uniform in black dinner suits while the women vied for attention in their couture dresses. It was hard not to be overwhelmed, and she was grateful for Alex's imperturbable presence by her side, the ease with which he drew her into conversation with the other guests.

She had discovered Sebastian Vaughn to be a gentle, soft-spoken man, his handsome face etched with lines of strain, his black hair already sprinkled with silver. Mindful of Madame Roussel's plea to help her grandson forget his problems for the evening, Jenna had done her best to help him relax, had chatted animatedly with him and persuaded him onto the dance floor. And she had been successful, Jenna decided with a satisfied smile, as she studied Seb's more relaxed features. During the course of the evening they had enjoyed several glasses of champagne, and their laughter, the way they sat with their heads close together, sharing a joke, had drawn comments from the other guests. Alex had managed to keep his thoughts to himself, but it was a close thing, he conceded as he watched Jenna lead his old friend onto the dance floor again. The tempo changed and Jenna slotted into Seb's arms and smiled up at him, seemingly oblivious to anyone else as they moved in perfect accord to the music. Jealousy was a rancid emotion, Alex discovered as he contemplated striding across the dance floor, wrenching Jenna away and rearranging Seb's good-looking features with his fist. Seb was one of his closest friends, for God's sake, a man who patently adored his wife, and Jenna had a husband—although it appeared that she had momentarily forgotten that fact.

'Seb, will you object if I steal my secretary for a moment?' Alex had been inundated with willing partners on the dance floor, and it had been relatively easy to manoeuvre a change-over, but Jenna immediately stepped away from his arms and smiled apologetically.

'Actually, I'm dying for a drink.' Anything was better than suffering the torture of dancing with Alex, praying that he didn't hear the pounding of her heart or notice the way her pulse raced. It would be agonisingly embarrassing if he should guess how much she wanted to rest her cheek against his chest, draw his head down and be kissed senseless.

'Another one?' Alex's brows rose as he escorted her to the bar. 'What would you like? Water or orange juice?'

'Well, I rather like champagne,' Jenna admitted with a giggle. She had never drunk champagne before, and it was a revelation: she felt happy and relaxed, and just the tiniest bit light-headed.

She couldn't understand why Alex looked so grim-faced. She had been aware of glowering looks from him all evening, when he hadn't been flirting with a variety of beautiful women. It was lucky she had been able to rely on Seb for company; Alex was in such demand that she might very easily have spent the evening as a wall-flower.

'I don't know what's the matter with you,' she said, staring dismally at the glass of iced water he handed her. 'We're supposed to be cheering Seb up.'

'You seem to be doing that all by yourself—although I'm not sure Madame Roussel meant for you to get blind drunk and seduce her grandson on the dance floor.'

'I am not drunk.' Somehow Alex had steered her out onto a large balcony, the blast of cold air making Jenna's head spin so that she grabbed hold of the balustrade. 'How dare you suggest that I was making a play for Seb? I was being friendly, that's all.'

'It looked a lot more than friendly from where I was standing. Your behaviour is the talk of the party. If you're determined to commit adultery, then do it with me. Seb has enough problems. The last thing Ellisa needs right now is to hear rumours that her husband had to fight off the attentions of a red-haired bimbo at his grandmother's party.'

Behind his sarcasm lurked blind fury, Jenna realised, and her own temper was instantly at boiling point; the crack of her hand against his cheek sounded like gunfire as it ricocheted around the balcony.

'I don't intend to commit adultery with anyone—least of all you,' she bit out, but beneath her bravado she felt horribly sick. She despised physical violence, but she had never felt so angry or humiliated in her life.

'Is that so? Then why have you been throwing out signals ever since we arrived in Paris? Don't try and deny it,' he said coldly. 'Every time I turn around I find those big grey eyes on me, inviting me, inciting me.'

'Inciting you to what? You're the one who keeps staring at me but tries to hide the fact whenever I look at you.'

'And you find that unsettling, do you? Maybe even embarrassing? Do you want to run home and tell Chris that your boss wants you in his bed?'

'No.' She stared at him miserably, tears burning behind her eyelids as she studied the livid handprint that stained his cheek. Her anger quickly dissipated to be replaced with shame. 'I want us to go back to being...friends.'

'We can never be friends,' he told her bluntly, and suddenly he was too close, his hands resting on the balustrade on either side of her body, caging her in although he did not touch her. 'And you know why.'

He lowered his head, his lips hovering millimetres above hers, so close that she could feel his warm breath on her skin, could count his eyelashes. His face was a sculpted mask, the skin drawn tight over prominent cheekbones, his eyes no longer cold, hard sapphires but burning with an intensity that caused an answering hunger to unfurl in the pit of her stomach. She had wanted this since the first time he had kissed her after Charles Metcalf's party, and suddenly her job, Lee, everything faded into insignificance as she faced up to the fact that she wanted *him*.

With helpless fascination she waited as his head lowered still further, until his mouth closed over hers, and with a stifled murmur of surrender she closed her eyes, giving herself up to pure sensation.

'Open your eyes,' he demanded. 'I want you to know it's me you're kissing.'

His mouth was hard, demanding her response, his tongue forcing entry between her lips with barely leashed savagery, as if determined to crush any sign of resistance. He need not have worried; she was powerless to prevent her response, her lips parting willingly under the pressure of his as the kiss went on and on, stoking a fire that was in danger of blazing out of control.

Still he did not touch her, his hands clenched so tightly around the balustrade that his knuckles were white, his face rigid with the effort of holding back, until with a groan he relaxed against her and she felt the glorious, rock-hard proof of his arousal. The effect was like pouring petrol onto a bonfire. She ran her hands over his chest with unashamed hunger, feeling the frantic thud of his heartbeat beneath her fingertips before winding her arms around his neck as if afraid that he might draw back.

'This is utter madness, but I can't fight it any more,' Alex muttered rawly. 'These past weeks I've been going mad watching you, wanting you, knowing that your husband is waiting for you at home.' His hands gripped her shoulders with bruising intensity as he fought an inward battle with himself, wanting to pull her close, but knowing that for sanity's sake he should push her away.

'He's not...' Jenna whispered. 'My husband... He's not at home...'

'You mean you've rowed? He's walked out on you? So what am I? The consolation prize?'

His fingers marked her skin, and she was sure her shoulders would break under the force of his grip. Her hands fell to her sides as she quailed beneath his contempt.

He stepped back from her and shook his head, sanity returning with a vengeance. 'I will not take responsibility for problems within your marriage, Jenna, and I will not act as a sop for your bruised ego. If Chris has walked out on you then quite frankly I don't blame him. You flirt with anything in trousers—look at your behaviour tonight with Seb. But if you're on the look-out for a rich meal ticket you can count me out.'

Jenna was incandescent with fury. To think she had felt guilty for slapping him, she raged silently. Right now she would happily beat him senseless. 'My husband hasn't left me... At least he did, but... Oh, it's all a muddle. How dare you accuse me of looking for a meal ticket? You kissed me; you made all the running.'

'And you were my poor, defenceless victim?' he mocked. 'Why don't we both be honest and admit that we fancy each other? Although a quick screw with my

OFFICIAL OPINION POLL

ANSWER 3 QUESTIONS AND WE'LL SEND YOU
2 FREE BOOKS AND A FREE GIFT!

0074823 |||█|||█|||| |||█|||| |||█|||| FREE GIFT CLAIM # 3953

DETACH AND MAIL CARD TODAY!

YOUR OPINION COUNTS!

Please check TRUE or FALSE below to express your opinion about the following statements:

Q1 Do you believe in "true love"?

"TRUE LOVE HAPPENS ONLY ONCE IN A LIFETIME."
- ○ TRUE
- ○ FALSE

Q2 Do you think marriage has any value in today's world?

"YOU CAN BE TOTALLY COMMITTED TO SOMEONE WITHOUT BEING MARRIED."
- ○ TRUE
- ○ FALSE

Q3 What kind of books do you enjoy?

"A GREAT NOVEL MUST HAVE A HAPPY ENDING."
- ○ TRUE
- ○ FALSE

YES, I have scratched the area below.

Please send me the 2 FREE BOOKS and FREE GIFT for which I qualify. I understand I am under no obligation to purchase any books, as explained on the back of this card.

306 HDL EFV7   106 HDL EFUW

FIRST NAME   LAST NAME

ADDRESS

APT.#   CITY

STATE/ PROV.   ZIP/POSTAL CODE

www.eHarlequin.com

(HTF-P-06/06)

The Harlequin Reader Service® — Here's how it works:

Accepting your 2 free books and mystery gift places you under no obligation to buy anything. You may keep the books and gift and return the shipping statement marked "cancel." If you do not cancel, about a month later we'll send you 6 additional books and bill you just $3.80 each in the U.S., or $4.47 each in Canada, plus 25¢ shipping & handling per book and applicable taxes if any.* That's the complete price and – compared to cover prices of $4.50 each in the U.S., and $5.25 each in Canada – it's quite a bargain! You may cancel at any time, but if you choose to continue, every month we'll send you 6 more books which you may either purchase at the discount price or return to us and cancel your subscription.

*Terms and prices subject to change without notice. Sales tax applicable in N.Y. Canadian residents will be charged applicable provincial taxes and GST.

If offer card is missing write to: The Harlequin Reader Service, 3010 Walden Ave., P.O. Box 1867, Buffalo, NY 14240-1867

BUSINESS REPLY MAIL
FIRST-CLASS MAIL   PERMIT NO. 717-003   BUFFALO, NY

POSTAGE WILL BE PAID BY ADDRESSEE

HARLEQUIN READER SERVICE
3010 WALDEN AVE
PO BOX 1867
BUFFALO NY 14240-9952

NO POSTAGE
NECESSARY
IF MAILED
IN THE
UNITED STATES

secretary has suddenly lost its appeal—you've got too much baggage.' He had swung away from her, but as he pushed open the door to re-enter the party he paused. 'One other thing—keep away from Seb. His life is enough of a mess as it is. He needs you like a hole in the head.'

Paris at night was a bustling mass of bright lights. At any other time Jenna would have been fascinated by the view from the window of the limousine that whisked them back to their hotel, but not tonight. Tonight she stared blankly ahead, determined not to be the one to break the icy silence, and beside her Alex seemed to share her intent. The tension between them was a tangible force.

The silence continued as they rode the lift up to the top floor of the hotel, and it took every inch of her will-power to keep from peeping in his direction, her fury palpable as she stalked ahead of him to the sanctuary of her room.

He was the most arrogant, conceited, infuriating man she had ever met, she fumed as she paced up and down her bedroom. How dared he imply that she had been flirting with Seb? Or, even worse, that she was actively hunting for a rich replacement husband? She hated him, she told herself, blinking back the sudden rush of tears. He hadn't hidden his contempt for her even as he'd played havoc with her emotions when he had kissed her. He might desire her in the most basic way, but he despised himself for what he saw as his weakness, and he despised her more.

She should have been honest from the start, she thought miserably. She should never have lied about Lee. But she had been so embarrassed on that first day, when she had made her attraction to Alex so obvious, that allowing him to believe she was happily married had been her only way of saving face. She was tempted to storm into his room and tell him the truth now, but if she explained that she was divorced wouldn't that just reinforce his belief that she was desperate for a rich meal ticket, as he had so delicately phrased it? Even worse, would he think she was available to sleep with him?

Her cheeks burned when she recalled the way she had melted with shameful eagerness in his arms. Her brain might dictate that she disliked him, but her body had a will of its own, and it was hungry for Alex Morrell. She wasn't the type to indulge in a one-night stand, she accepted honestly, but Alex wasn't offering anything else. Even if by some miracle he decided that he wanted a proper relationship with her, there was Maisie to consider, and she could just picture his horror if she turned up on a date with her small daughter in tow.

It was past midnight, but she was too wound up to sleep as she replayed Alex's words over and over in her mind. His taunt that she was a bimbo really stung, and she glared at her reflection in the mirror, noting with disgust her flushed cheeks and the way the black dress clung to her curves, emphasising the fullness of her breasts and her slender waist. He had been the one to demand that she get dolled up, but when she had followed his instructions he had more or less accused her of being a tart.

There was no pleasing some people, she decided irritably as she flipped open her laptop. She still had a pile of notes to type up—a task Alex had suggested she leave until the morning. But presumably the quicker Seb's case was sewn up, the quicker they could go home. She was determined to prove that she was the most efficient, conscientious *bimbo* Alex Morrell had ever met, and she would enjoy his expression when she informed him first thing tomorrow morning that all her work was up to date.

*   *   *

The knock on the interconnecting door between her room and Alex's brought her head up, and she glanced at her watch, startled to find that she had been working for over an hour. The knock came again, louder and more forceful, and with a sigh she marched over to the door.

'What do you want?' she demanded coolly, determined not to be fazed by the sight of Alex lounging in the doorway. He had discarded his tie and unfastened several shirt buttons, so that the tanned column of his throat was exposed, and she hastily focused on a point over his shoulder.

'You're dressed,' he commented, sounding surprised, and she glared at him.

'What did you expect? I'm not in the habit of answering my door stark naked.'

'What a wonderful picture that evokes,' he murmured, resting his hands on either side of the doorframe so that she felt swamped by his raw masculinity and took a step backwards.

'Have you been drinking?' she accused, catching the faint smell of whisky on his breath, and he shrugged.

'I may have had a couple, to drown my sorrows, but I'm not drunk. I saw the light from beneath your bedroom door and thought you'd fallen asleep with the lamp on. It's past one in the morning,' he added with another puzzled glance at her fully dressed form. 'What are you doing?'

'Working. I've just finished typing up the notes for Seb's case.'

'I didn't mean for you to do that now.'

'I thought it would leave me the morning free to chase prospective sugar daddies. It's hard work being a bimbo, you know.'

'Ah.' Alex had the grace to look shamefaced. 'That's

the real reason I'm here.' He strolled through the doorway and paced her room restlessly, picking up and setting down items on her dressing table until her nerves were on edge.

'Well, come in—make yourself at home,' she snapped, and he sighed and raked a hand through his hair.

'You're not going to make this easy for me, are you? I'm trying to apologise,' he added impatiently, when she could not disguise her puzzlement.

'Oh, I see.'

'I was unforgivably rude and insulting. Watching you cosy up to Seb brought out my jealous streak, I'm afraid.'

'I wasn't doing anything with him,' Jenna argued. 'And even if I had been, you have no right to question my behaviour.'

'No,' he conceded heavily. 'That right belongs to your husband.' He glanced down at her laptop and shook his head. 'I can't believe you've been working at this time of night.'

'It was either that or throw something—preferably at your head,' Jenna admitted, and her eyes scanned his face, searching for any sign of injury where she had slapped him. She abhorred violence of any kind, and, faced with his apology, she felt even more ashamed of her loss of temper. 'I'm sorry I slapped you—even though you did ask for it,' she added, and was startled by his sudden laughter.

'That's my girl. Determined to have the last word.'

Suddenly the room seemed heavy with tension, and Jenna couldn't repress a quiver of response to his softly spoken words.

'I'm not your girl,' she pointed out huskily.

'I guess not.' He had moved without her being aware of it, and now stood so close that he overwhelmed her.

He had switched off the overhead light and the room was bathed in the gentle glow from one of the ornate bedside lamps. A lock of hair fell across his forehead, lending him a rakish air that only emphasised his sexiness, and she felt her breath snag in her throat as he reached out and stroked her hair back from her face. Instantly her senses were on high alert, so that she was acutely aware of the heat emanating from his body and the sensual musk of his cologne. She watched their reflection in the dressing-table mirror, noting how he towered over her, big and faintly menacing, his hands dark against the whiteness of her skin. But it was not him she was afraid of. It was herself and her wayward response to him.

'You should go,' she whispered thickly, and heard him sigh, felt his fingers slide through her hair and then stop, the sudden tension that gripped him instantly transmuting to her.

'I hurt you,' he said quietly, and she followed his gaze to the faint marks on her upper arms.

Quickly she tried to move away, but he stalled her, and she felt him ease the zip of her dress down a little, enabling him to push the straps away so that he could view the marks. His eyes were dark with a mixture of regret and self-disgust, and she urgently sought to reassure him.

'I bruise easily.'

'Do you? Is that the excuse you give when your husband marks you?' He brushed her hair from her temple, the bruise on her forehead a stark reminder that he had acted no better than the man she had married.

'You were angry—' she began, and his head came up, his eyes flashing fire.

'And that's an excuse?' he bit out furiously, his anger directed solely at himself. 'I have never used any kind of violent force on a woman. And you—you're so tiny, so fragile I could crush your bones in my grasp. That doesn't make it right. I'm not proud of losing my temper.' His voice was so low it caressed her skin, and he lowered his head, his mouth moving in gentle contrition over the bruises on her arms.

Her dress slithered lower and for a second he hesitated, and then he reached behind her and slowly drew her zip down the length of her spine. Jenna discovered that she couldn't move, could barely breathe, her gaze locked with his as the bodice fell to her waist, revealing the black lacy bra he had bought her, and she swallowed when he traced his fingers down to the valley between her breasts.

'I'm sorry I hurt you.' His husky whisper feathered across her skin and she could hear the remorse in his voice.

'It's all right.' He seemed curiously vulnerable, stripped of his wonderful arrogance, and she ached for him, anxious to offer him forgiveness. 'I know you didn't mean to hurt me.'

'Hurting you is the last thing I want to do.' The room was so quiet she could hear the thud of her heart, of his, and for a second he hesitated, his gaze locked with hers before he uttered a low groan, his hand moving down to tug the skirt of her dress so that it fell in a pool of black silk at her feet.

'You are exquisite,' he breathed, his hands skimming her slender waist, her scantily cut lace panties, and coming to rest at the tops of her stockings.

Her stiletto heels made her legs seem even longer—she looked sexy and seductive, she realised with a shock, as she studied her semi-naked body in the mirror. Her hair fell over one shoulder and her eyelids felt heavy; there was a sultry gleam in her eyes that she could not disguise, and she made no demur when he drew her in his arms.

'I want you,' he admitted thickly. 'But you know that, don't you?'

Jenna said nothing. She seemed to have lost all power of speech, could only stare up at him, mesmerised by the sheer hunger in his eyes, her body jerking in response to the rigid set of his jaw as he fought for control. She wanted him to kiss her, wanted it so much she would surely die with wanting, and, unable to wait any longer, she stretched up on tiptoe to close the gap between them. She cupped her hands round his face, the faint stubble rough against her skin as she brought his mouth down to hers and initiated a kiss that stirred his soul.

Almost instantly he sought to take control, his mouth moving over hers, deepening the pressure, until she clung to him, his willing captive, while he continued his flagrant assault on her senses.

For a moment the room spun, and Jenna clung to Alex's shoulders as he lifted her and moved over to the bed, depositing her on the sheets and instantly coming down beside her. He dominated her senses; there was no room in her mind for any other thought than him and her desperate need to be even closer to him, to feel him skin on skin. She fumbled with his shirt buttons, sighing her pleasure when at last she was able to push the material over his shoulders.

He had a fantastic body, powerful and muscular, as befitted a man who excelled at a variety of sports in his leisure time. She could feel the hardness of his arousal straining against his trousers, and with an impatient movement he tugged at the zip and shrugged out of them, so that his only covering was a pair of black silk boxers. The feel of his hair-roughened thighs pressing against her caused liquid heat to pool between her legs. She felt as if time was suspended and there was nothing but now, this moment and Alex. Only when she felt his fingers dip beneath her bra, easing the material aside to reveal her breast, did she open her eyes, the slumberous heat in his making her shiver with desire.

He deliberately held her gaze before lowering his head, and the feel of his mouth on her breast caused her to cry out as his tongue lapped the sensitive peak and a shaft of pleasure unfurled in the pit of her stomach.

'Tell me you want me as much as I want you.' Alex's voice grazed her skin as his mouth trailed a fiery path to her navel. 'I want to know that it's me you're thinking of when we make love, not your husband. You don't have to stay tied to a man who hurts you,' he went on inexorably, ignoring the panic in her eyes as reality intruded. 'There's no unbreakable bond between you.'

Now was the time to tell him that she was no longer married, that she was a free agent, Jenna accepted. She wanted him with an emotion akin to desperation, with a hunger she had never experienced before, certainly not with Lee—but if she admitted that fact where would it leave her? At best all Alex wanted was a brief affair, and when it was over would he expect her to leave her job, or would she be like Katrin Jefferstone, unable to hide her feelings for him and an object of pity?

She had too much pride for that, Jenna acknowledged, and there was too much else at stake. Where would Maisie fit into the equation if she embarked on a relationship with Alex? And how much more leverage would it give Lee if he decided to fight for custody of their daughter?

'There is a bond between us that will last a lifetime,' she whispered, desire retreating and leaving in its wake emptiness and shame. She was linked to Lee inextricably—not through love, but through Maisie, the daughter Alex knew nothing about.

Alex rolled onto his side and she shivered at the coldness in his eyes. 'In that case what the hell are you playing at by inviting me into your bed? If you were hoping to snag a wealthy lover as well as your husband, think again. Chris might be willing to share, but I'm damn well not.'

He swung his legs over the side of the bed and pulled on his trousers with jerky, economical movements that betrayed his bitterness, the contempt in his eyes crucifying her as his gaze roamed her body in insolent appraisal.

'I didn't invite you,' Jenna defended herself. 'You came into my room. You started this.'

'It was hardly against your will,' Alex snapped scathingly. 'You made your enthusiasm abundantly clear. But I at least retain some morals, and I'm afraid I must turn down what's all too clearly on offer.'

With infuriating calm he eased her bra back into place, and even then, knowing how much he despised her, she was unable to disguise her shiver as his fingers brushed against her breast.

'Thanks, but no thanks,' he taunted as he crossed the room, and Jenna shot after him, slamming the interconnecting door after him and bolting it as if barricading herself from all the demons in hell.

CHAPTER SIX

ON THEIR return flight to England Alex was aloof to the point of totally ignoring her, and Jenna quailed beneath his icy disdain on the few occasions he deemed it necessary to speak to her.

He was in court for the rest of the week, and she did not dare enquire on the outcome of Sebastian Vaughn's case—although she later learned from Margaret that Seb had escaped a criminal record and been bound over to keep the peace.

The stand-off carried into the following week, and Alex's coldness towards her and his biting sarcasm was not going unnoticed by the other staff.

'Heaven knows what you've done to upset Alex,' Katrin snapped as she swept past Jenna's desk. 'I've never known him in such a foul mood.'

'Why assume that his mood has anything to do with me?' Jenna argued stubbornly, refusing to be browbeaten. Alex's scathing tongue was enough to contend with; she certainly didn't need Katrin getting in on the act.

'Because he's been like it ever since the two of you returned from Paris. I hope you didn't embarrass him. The Vaughns are a very high-profile family.'

By the end of that week Jenna was ready to call it a day. There had to be other jobs, she argued as she spilled out of the overcrowded tube train at London Bridge and headed towards the Morrell and Partners offices. The atmosphere at work was truly awful, and Alex's bad temper was affecting everyone. For the sake of the other members of staff as well as her own sanity she would have to leave—and right now. Pole dancing in a sleazy nightclub seemed preferable to suffering another day of Alex's vicious tongue.

There was an air of fevered speculation in the offices, and Jenna could not hide her curiosity as she reached her desk. 'Has something happened?' she asked one of the juniors.

'You mean you haven't heard? Alex is getting married to Selina Carter-Lloyd; their engagement was announced in the papers this morning.'

For a moment the floor rocked beneath her feet, and she actually gripped the edge of her desk, fighting for composure. 'Well, that is news,' she said quietly. 'Totally out of the blue.'

'I know—it's amazing, isn't it? Alex is such a dark horse. Not even Margaret knew until this morning,' the junior confided excitedly. 'Do you think that's the reason he's been in such a bad mood recently? Maybe he and Miss Carter-Lloyd had an argument, but they've obviously made up now. It's so romantic. He's coming along the corridor now. I'm going to congratulate him.'

Jenna took advantage of the younger girl's excitement to escape to the cloakroom, where she forced herself to comb her hair and check her make-up with fingers that trembled.

Katrin stepped out of one of the cubicles, her face so pale that her scarlet lipstick cut a vivid slash across her face, her eyes hollow with misery. In the midst of her own shock Jenna felt a wave of sympathy for the other woman, and she put a hand on Katrin's arm.

'Katrin, I'm sorry.'

'For what?' Katrin surveyed her with haughty disdain, her lip curling. 'Do you think I care? It's you I feel sorry for. Do you think I hadn't noticed your pathetic crush on Alex? The way you sit mooning over him like some lovesick teenager? He's out of your reach now, that's for sure.'

It was sheer dogged pride that saw Jenna walk into Alex's office and congratulate him on his engagement in a cool, uninterested tone. But for a man in love he didn't look very happy, she noted when he turned away from the window to survey her with cold blue eyes, his expression unfathomable.

'You and Selina must be busy making arrangements,' she murmured. 'When is the wedding?'

'In the spring. We haven't set a date yet,' came the brusque reply. 'We've put the planning on hold for a few weeks. As you know, Selina is a sports journalist with a magazine. She's flying to Durban next week, to cover a series of polo matches, and I want her to honour her commitment. It'll give her a chance to decide whether marrying me is really what she wants to do.'

He couldn't admit that he had insisted on Selina going to South Africa, or that he needed the reprieve while he came to terms with an engagement that he had regretted the minute the words had left his mouth. He was thirty-eight, he reminded himself. It was high time he settled down and produced the grandchildren his parents so hoped for. Marriage to Selina was the sensible option. He couldn't pretend that he was madly in love with her, but he liked her, and a marriage built on a foundation of respect and mutual goals was infinitely more desirable than one that involved messy emotions.

He suspected that Jenna's marriage was far from happy, yet for reasons he couldn't fathom she insisted that she had made a lifetime commitment to her husband. In a climate of increasing divorce statistics he supposed he should applaud her loyalty but as he stared at her he recalled the bruise on her face and fought an overwhelming urge to pull her into his arms and tell her that he would take care of her.

She didn't want his protection, he reminded himself. She desired him—even now she was unable to disguise the flare of hunger in her eyes before her lashes swept down to conceal her emotions—but she didn't want him with any degree of permanency in her life, and he was past the age of happily settling for a role as her stud.

'I'm sure Selina is already convinced that she wants to marry you,' Jenna said quietly, taken aback by the hint of uncertainty in Alex's voice. 'But you're right. Marriage is a huge step.'

'You're the expert, so you should know.'

Across the office his eyes burned into hers, and she trembled at the unspoken message in those deep blue depths. He moved to stand in front of her, so close it would take one tiny step to reach the sanctuary of his arms, and she was tempted, so tempted that every fibre of her being yearned to close the gap between them. The air thrummed with tension, the silence so intense she could hear the pounding of her heart.

'It's not too late,' he offered huskily, his eyes never leaving hers, and she bit down hard on her lip, tasted blood as she waged an inner battle.

Go to him, hope he would accept Maisie, and in doing so wreck his engagement to the woman who would make him an ideal wife? Or walk away from what was never going to be anything more than a temporary affair, where she stood to lose her self-respect, her job, and possibly her child?

She loved him, she acknowledged painfully. This wasn't just about desire or sex. Somewhere along the line she had fallen in love with Alex, with his wit, his charm, his strength, and above all his sense of honour.

But Alex used his formidable skill in the courtroom to champion the underdog. He believed that marriage should be a lifelong commitment, particularly if children were involved, yet if Lee had his way she was going to be embroiled in a bitter custody battle for Maisie. Where would Alex's sympathies lie? she wondered. Any sort of relationship with her would necessitate a relationship with her daughter, because the two of them came as a package, yet Alex did not even know of Maisie's existence. It would be better for all of them if he never knew, if he went ahead with his marriage to Selina, whom he presumably loved, and forgot this fierce attraction that burned between them. In a matter of weeks, months at the most, it would have burned itself out; it would be better for all of them if they never lit the fuse.

'We met at the wrong time, Alex; it's too late for both of us. You have a wonderful future ahead of you. Selina will make you an ideal wife and I hope you'll both be very happy.'

'As happy as you?' he queried softly, drawing his thumb-pad lightly over her lips and discovering a smear of blood on his skin. 'God, Jenna!'

His frustration spilled over and he pulled her into his arms, but his mouth was gentle on hers, caressing her tender flesh, the kiss so sweetly beguiling that she had no thought but to respond. He forced himself to relax, to explore her mouth with a slow sensuality, waiting until he felt her lips part before sliding his tongue into her and savouring her inner warmth.

He drew back at last, when his body felt taut with a need he dared not reveal, and sensing his withdrawal she stepped back, his gentle kiss on her forehead a final benediction. He was saying goodbye.

The next few weeks were torturous, and Jenna took to scanning the appointments pages of the newspapers, in the hope of finding another job that paid as well as her position at Morrell and Partners.

November dragged into December, the leaden skies echoing the feeling around her heart, and all the while she and Alex skirted around one another like moths drawn to a flame, but determined not to singe their wings. Fortunately he was in court for much of the time, working on a lengthy fraud trial, but she suspected that his new habit of e-mailing the office from home was so that he could avoid her.

Midway through another dismal week he announced that he was joining Selina in Durban for a few days, and took the ribbing that he was having his honeymoon before the wedding with good grace. Although, had she dared look into his eyes, Jenna would have seen that his smile did not reach them.

Jenna had given up hope that the sun would ever shine again, and for once was glad of the incessant rain. Lee had phoned to say that he intended to take Maisie out for the day on Saturday, possibly to the zoo, and as Jenna listened to the storm raging on Friday night she assumed that he would ring to cancel.

Saturday dawned cold but bright, and her heart sank as the peal of the doorbell heralded his arrival, her hands shaking as she fastened the buttons of Maisie's coat.

'I want you to come, Mummy.' Maisie's lip wobbled ominously, her grey eyes glistening like silvery pools, and Jenna sought to control her own emotions as she reassured the little girl.

'You're going to have a lovely time with Daddy, I promise. He loves you very much, Maisie, and I'll be here, waiting for you when you come back.' The second was a certainty; she would be counting the hours until Lee brought Maisie safely home. Of the first, she wasn't convinced. But Lee was Maisie's father, she had to give him the benefit of the doubt.

'How many children are you taking to the zoo?' she queried faintly when Lee led the way to a top-of-the-range people carrier fitted with eight seats.

'Louise thought we should have a big car for all Maisie's gear,' he explained.

'What gear? She's not a kit of parts, you know, just one small child—and who's Louise?'

'Louise is my fiancée. She can't wait to meet my little girl, especially when she's such a pretty little thing,' Lee said, his satisfaction with Maisie's appearance evident. 'She's been buying things for weeks—toys, clothes, a pushchair.'

'Maisie's too big for a pushchair,' Jenna argued, and Lee threw her an impatient look.

'Just leave it, Jenna. Louise has been looking forward to meeting Maisie for a long time; she's bound to want to spoil her.'

She couldn't find fault with the top-quality safety seat, Jenna acknowledged as Lee strapped Maisie in, but neither could she throw off her feeling of unease as she watched the car pull away.

After pacing the house for an hour she was persuaded by a concerned Chris to go shopping, her brother's promise to stay by the phone and call her if Lee reported any problems alleviating her worry slightly.

'I see Lee's fallen on his feet with that girlfriend of his.'

Jenna had been staring blankly at a shop window full of Christmas decorations when a familiar voice sounded in her ear and she turned to see her neighbour, Lee's old friend from the fire station, Brian Wells.

'Nice motor he was driving this morning. Taken Maisie out for the day, has he?'

'Yes.' Jenna's tone was cool. She had never liked Brian, never been taken in by his overt friendliness—particularly when he had always taken delight in patting various parts of her anatomy, mainly her bottom, when she had been coerced by Lee to socialise with him and his wife Ann. 'You don't miss much, do you, Brian?'

'Not a lot,' Brian informed her with sly grin. 'Lee asked me to keep an eye on you—friendly like, you know. Where's your posh bloke with the Ferrari? Dumped you, has he?'

Jenna felt sick. 'Lee asked you to spy on me?' No wonder he always seemed to know her movements; no wonder the disturbing phone calls always occurred after she had been out on an occasional date. Brian had been watching her and reporting back to Lee.

'Not spying,' Brian's wife hastily interposed. 'Lee was worried about you living in the house on your own, and of course he was concerned about Maisie.'

'Oh, of course,' Jenna agreed cynically. 'So concerned he's hardly bothered with her up until now.'

'Well, now he wants to marry Louise,' Ann admitted, and Jenna frowned. 'What does that have to do with Maisie?'

'Louise is very well off. She runs her own company— a dating agency.'

'And she selected Lee for herself? Goodness, her business must be a roaring success. But I still don't understand.'

'Louise can't have children,' Ann explained, her eyes on Jenna, so that she didn't notice the warning glare from her husband. 'She's mid-forties now, and it seems that she's unlikely to ever fall pregnant. She feels she devoted so many years to her career she sacrificed her chances of having a baby, or so Lee says.'

'So Lee's plan is to provide her with a child—my child—in return for marriage and a meal ticket for life?'

'I wouldn't put it quite like that,' Brian remonstrated. 'Lee's main concern is that Maisie is brought up in a stable environment, and you must admit introducing her to a steady stream of your boyfriends is hardly ideal.'

'I don't have a stream of boyfriends. I don't even have a trickle. And you can tell Lee that I refuse to stand by and allow his girlfriend to play happy families with my daughter.'

'She's his daughter too,' Brian reminded her. 'Maybe the courts will decide that Maisie will be better cared for by her daddy and his new wife.'

'He'll never get away with it,' Jenna told Chris later, as she paced the living room.

'Course he won't,' Chris agreed sagely. 'Even if the girlfriend pays out for top lawyers, you can still prove that Lee hasn't taken any interest in Maisie up till now, and certainly never paid any maintenance.'

Jenna was not reassured, and fretted all afternoon, relief flooding through her when the people carrier pulled up outside the house.

'What on earth is she wearing?' she demanded when Maisie trotted through the front door looking like a fluffy marshmallow in a confection of pink fur.

'Auntie Louise bought you a new coat and hat, didn't

she?' Lee said, hastily handing his daughter over as she waved a sticky lollipop near his jacket.

'She's got a perfectly good winter coat,' Jenna argued furiously. 'Maisie's not a doll, Lee. Your girlfriend might want a ready-made family, but she's not having mine.'

'We'll see, won't we?' Lee murmured, and pulled a piece of paper from his pocket.

It was a cheque made out to Jenna, and her eyebrows shot up as she stared at the amount detailed. 'What's this for?'

'I fell a bit behind with maintenance for Maisie. That should cover what I owe.'

Jenna stared at the cheque and felt the cold hand of fear close around her heart. Lee meant business, she realised sickly. He intended to fight for custody of Maisie and his first step was to prove that he was a caring and responsible father.

'I'll fight you all the way,' she warned her ex-husband bitterly. 'If you want to see Maisie and build a proper relationship with her, that's fine. I would never prevent her from seeing her father. But you are not going to use her as bargaining counter in order to gain a rich wife.'

Lee had the grace to look shamefaced for all of two seconds. 'As they say in the movies, I'll see you in court,' he said confidently, and as he walked towards the door he stepped on her foot.

'Ow! Careful.' Jenna winced and Lee glanced down, then deliberately ground his boot into her bare foot. 'Lee, you're hurting me.'

'Oops! Sorry! Silly Daddy trod on Mummy's foot,' he said, with a laugh for Maisie's benefit, and Jenna blinked back tears of real pain.

'You bastard,' she whispered. 'Try any more tricks like that and I'll report you for assault.'

Lee's good-looking face split into a grin as he sauntered out of the door. 'It was an accident, baby. I'd like to see you prove otherwise.'

The following week Jenna's foot was still black, and she hobbled into work, cursing Lee and his spite. But she forgot her problems for a moment when she discovered Margaret in tears.

'It's John,' Margaret confided as she mopped her eyes. 'His condition is deteriorating and I don't know if I can manage like this for much longer. Yesterday he heated up a can of soup in the microwave, and of course it exploded everywhere. While I was clearing up the mess he slipped out of the back door and was found wandering along the high street wearing his pyjamas.'

'I thought he was attending a day center?' Jenna murmured sympathetically.

'He does go on weekdays, while I'm at work, but it's up to me to look after him in the evenings and weekends, and now Alex has asked me to go to Yorkshire with him.'

'Well, I'll go instead. I thought that was one of my duties anyway.'

'You and Alex don't seem to be getting on very well at the moment,' Margaret explained. 'The date for Alex's client's court appearance was changed at the last minute, and I offered to travel up to York with him.'

'Leave it with me,' Jenna said briskly, and made a hurried phone call to her neighbour Nora, to ask if she could care for Maisie for the night. 'It's an emergency,' she explained to Nora. 'I know Maisie will be happy staying with you, but I'm worried about Lee finding out. He'll be sure to accuse me of abandoning her.'

'Don't worry about that little toad; if he comes here he'll get short shrift from me,' Nora replied stoutly.

'You're an excellent mother, Jenna, but Lee always did knock your confidence. It's about time you stood up to him.'

Alex was already waiting in the car, Margaret told her, but as Jenna approached the Bentley she was surprised to see him sitting in the driver's seat, rather than his chauffeur.

'Barton has the flu, so I'm driving,' he explained. 'I'd actually intended to fly, but the weather reports for the north are atrocious. Where's Margaret?'

Swiftly Jenna detailed the reason for the change of plan and Alex studied her in silence for a moment. 'You don't have anything with you,' he pointed out. 'And it'll be too late to drive back tonight.'

'There must be shops in Yorkshire, Alex. I'll buy a toothbrush and anything else I need when we arrive. Why do you need to go to York anyway?' she asked as he negotiated the busy London streets.

'My client's committal hearing is in court there—although the trial will eventually take place at the Old Bailey. It's a murder trial,' he added. 'Jason Doyle was allegedly stabbed to death by his wife. By all accounts it was a violent relationship, and he often beat her. It appears that she couldn't take his drunken rages any more.'

'And you're prosecuting Mr Doyle's wife?' Jenna queried, trying to suppress a shudder. Lee had never used his fists on her, but how many more 'accidents' would she suffer when he was around?

Alex threw her a glance, his curiosity aroused by the forceful emotion in her voice. 'No, I'm defending Susan Doyle. The poor woman has had a terrible life; I just hope I can arrange bail.'

They arrived in York mid-afternoon and went straight to the magistrates court. Snow had been falling across the northern counties all day, and by early evening the roads around the city were gridlocked.

'We're booked into a hotel on the outskirts of town,' Alex said, his impatience tangible as they sat in a queue of traffic. 'If we turn off at the next junction we should be able to follow a loop around the city and reach the hotel that way. Here—take the map.'

Forty-five minutes later Alex's temper was as filthy as the weather, and he cursed as he peered through the windscreen, his vision rapidly impeded by the snow that was falling faster than the wipers could cope with.

'Where the hell are we? I'm sure we've come too far away from the town and we're heading onto the moors.'

'Take the next right,' Jenna advised as she frantically scanned the map.

'Are you sure? York's to the left of us—I can see lights in the distance and I'm going to head towards them.'

'The map says turn right,' Jenna insisted, but then gave up. She was all too familiar with Alex's stubborn streak and deemed it wiser to say nothing as the road grew narrower and his impatience became a palpable force.

The wind whipped the snow into drifts, the road no more than a cart track now, while all around the darkness closed in on them. Eventually Alex cut the engine.

'This is hopeless; I'm going to turn back before we get snowed in,' he growled, his tone plainly accusing.

'I told you to turn right—you're the one who decided you knew better than the map, in typical pig-headed fashion,' Jenna snapped furiously. 'I am capable of reading a map, you know!'

'Fine, so it's my fault we're lost?'

'If you hadn't been so impatient we could have just sat in the traffic jam for a few minutes. We'd be at the hotel now, instead of struggling to find our way out of a snow-storm.'

Alex muttered under his breath and attempted to turn the car around, but the wheels spun on the icy road so that he lost control and they slithered backwards into a ditch.

'Terrific, we're well and truly stranded,' he reported, after climbing out of the car to inspect the situation. 'The back end's right in the ditch. You'd better get out in case the car slides any further.'

An icy blast of air hit Jenna as she opened the car door, her feet sinking into a snowdrift at least a foot deep. 'What are we going to do?' she asked as Alex waved his mobile phone in the air, trying to locate a signal.

'Walk, I suppose. Even if I could ring for roadside assistance nothing's going to be able to get down this narrow track until daylight.'

'Maybe we should just wait in the car,' Jenna said, with a fearful glance across the dark fields at the rapidly mounting snow.

'For what?' Alex snapped witheringly as he reached onto the back seat of the car for his overnight bag. 'Lassie? A Saint Bernard with a barrel of brandy around its neck? We'll head back up the lane. I'm sure we passed a pub a few miles back.'

'A few miles?' Jenna repeated faintly as she picked her way through the snow, trying to keep close to Alex who held the torch.

Within minutes it was obvious that her thin coat was totally inadequate for the wintry conditions, and she struggled to keep her balance in her high-heeled boots, her bruised foot aching with the effort.

'Come on—keep up,' Alex ordered after they had been walking for ten minutes, his tone impatient as he flicked a beam of torchlight over her bedraggled form, his frown deepening when he noticed her limping. 'What's the matter with your foot?'

'Nothing—apart from frostbite.' She stumbled to a halt in front of him and he tilted her chin to stare into her eyes, his sixth sense alerted by a nuance in her voice.

'Let me guess—you walked into another door?'

Jenna sighed. 'I dropped something on my foot and bruised it, that's all.'

'It must have been something extremely heavy, you can hardly walk. What was it?'

Jenna was too cold and tired to think straight, let alone come up with a suitable lie to placate Alex, and she stared at him in silence.

'If your husband values his life, don't ever allow him anywhere near me,' he bit out violently, his jaw rigid as he fought to contain his anger.

For the life of him he couldn't understand why she remained in a marriage that was at best unhappy and at worst placed her in physical danger from her husband. He had spent hours listening to his client, who stood accused of murdering her husband, horrified by the litany of abuse she had suffered for years at the hands of the man who had purportedly loved her, and he felt sick when he imagined Jenna in a similar situation.

His anger sent him striding on ahead, but minutes later he realised that she was no longer following him and turned back.

'I can't walk any further,' Jenna whispered as she sat huddled on the stone wall that ran alongside the road. 'You'll have to go on without me.'

'Don't be ridiculous. Do you really think I'd just abandon you in the middle of nowhere?' She looked small and fragile, her eyes blinking at him like a startled doe in the light from the torch, and he felt a hand squeeze his heart. 'I'm not leaving you, sweetheart, so either we both sit here and freeze or you hold my hand and we keep going until we reach civilisation.'

With her fingers curled around his big hand they battled on, until Jenna could barely lift one foot in front of the other. She was too exhausted to offer any resistance when he lifted her into his arms and carried her to the door of an isolated pub.

The landlord was a true Yorkshireman, who welcomed them inside and stoked the fire until it roared, urging them to warm themselves while he called his wife.

'I can't believe anyone's out on a night like this,' she said as she bustled in from the kitchen with hot drinks, and Jenna smiled weakly, her body limp as it acclimatised to the warm pub after the freezing temperature outside.

She closed her eyes and let Alex explain the details of how they had become lost, only opening them again when the room swayed and she found herself clasped against his chest once more.

'At least we've a bed for the night,' he murmured as he climbed the stairs. 'The landlady, Mrs Pike, said to use the room at the far end of the landing. She's gone to find you some dry clothes,' he added as he deposited Jenna in the centre of a small bedroom which was dominated by a very large bed.

'Where's your room?' Jenna queried tiredly as she flopped down on the bed. The mattress felt gloriously soft, and her eyelids drifted shut, but she forced them open again as she felt a hand tug the zip of her boots.

'You need to get out of these wet things,' Alex told her firmly. 'You're blue with cold; I wouldn't be surprised if you've got hypothermia.'

'I'm okay, Alex. I can manage,' Jenna squeaked, slapping away the hands that were busily unfastening her coat buttons. 'I asked you where you're going to sleep tonight.'

'In here,' he replied calmly, and she frowned.

'So where's my room?'

'This is it—one room, and by the looks of it one bed. What did you expect? The Hilton?'

Jenna's tiredness miraculously vanished, and she glared at Alex. 'I'm not sharing a bed with you,' she informed him coldly, but at that moment Mrs Pike tapped on the door, smiling cheerfully as she handed Jenna a voluminous cotton nightdress.

'Here you are, pet; your husband explained that you left all your belongings in the car. It's a raw night, and no mistake, you'll have to snuggle up close to him and keep warm.'

CHAPTER SEVEN

JENNA rolled onto her side on the ancient sofa and cursed beneath her breath as her hip ground against an unruly spring. The two-seater sofa was upholstered in a curious material—horsehair wouldn't have surprised her—and as she wriggled to find a comfortable spot her blanket slithered to the floor.

'Alex, are you awake?' No sound came from the bed, which only increased her irritation. He must have fallen straight to sleep—but then he had the luxury of the double bed to himself, while she was forced to manage on this sofa which was practically an antique.

Not that Alex had *made* her sleep on the sofa, she admitted honestly.

'It's a big enough bed for the two of us,' he had argued, after flatly refusing to take the sofa himself. 'For heaven's sake, Jenna, I've wrecked my car and battled through a blizzard. My libido is the last thing that's troubling me, and the sight of you in that nightdress does not incite my lust, I can assure you.'

'I'm not sharing a bed with you, and that's final,' Jenna had snapped as she'd snatched a pillow and blanket and headed for the sofa. 'I'd rather cuddle up with a rattlesnake.'

'Please yourself,' he had murmured, beginning to unbutton his shirt, and as his hands had reached for the zip of his trousers she'd given a yelp of impotent fury and hurried to the bathroom.

It was freezing, she thought grumpily as she wrapped

the folds of the enormous nightdress around her. She was tired, cold and miserable, and she hated Alex Morrell— but her reluctance to share his bed had little to do with fear that he would use the situation to his own advantage. As he had pointed out, the sight of her looking as though she had stepped from the pages of *Little Women* did nothing to trigger his desire, but unfortunately one glance at his naked chest had sent her hormones into overdrive. It was herself she didn't trust.

The sound of his contented sigh as he rolled over was too much to bear, and she sat up and punched her pillow into submission. 'God, he sleeps like the dead,' she muttered, and in the darkness Alex grinned.

Another few minutes and he would have to take charge of the situation, by picking her up and placing her in the bed, if necessary. But as he lay still he heard her move, and the mattress depressed slightly as she slid beneath the sheets.

The bed had to be as old as the sofa, Jenna decided as she hooked her fingers round the edge of the mattress to prevent herself from rolling into the dip in its centre. It was blissfully warm, though. She could feel the heat that emanated from Alex's body and shifted further to her side of the bed, away from temptation. It would be like spending the night clinging to the north face of the Eiger, she decided, as she hung on to the mattress.

But gradually her grip relaxed, and, left to its own devices, her body rolled towards Alex and curled into the crook of his arm.

It was still dark when Jenna awoke, but moonlight filtered through the gap in the curtains and cast shadows over the room. She was warm and comfortable, but as she stretched she came into contact with something hard, and when she turned her head she discovered she was lying in Alex's arms.

She should move, a warning voice sounded in her subconscious. But he was still asleep, what harm would it do to steal a few moments of pleasure? In sleep his stern features appeared more relaxed, and she stared at him, absorbing the sheer beauty of his bone structure, the chiselled contours of his face and the resolute strength of his chin. The sheet lay across his chest and she couldn't prevent her fingers from pushing it lower, to reveal the whorls of dark hair that arrowed down to his hips.

She should stop, the warning voice told her. But the temptation to push the sheet even lower was too strong, and she held her breath, listening to his and watching the even rise and fall of his chest.

'God, you're a fidget!'

The sheet was halfway down his hip, and her hand trembled as she flicked it back into place, her eyes huge with mortification, guilt, and an elemental hunger she couldn't disguise.

'How long have you been awake?' she whispered accusingly, and his mouth curved into a lazy smile.

'Long enough.'

'What must you think of me?' she muttered thickly, and he slid his hand into her hair to prevent her from escaping.

'I think that this has gone on long enough,' he told her rawly, the silence of the room so intense that the ticking of the clock sounded as thunderous as her pounding heart. 'I think you've finally come to realise, as I have, that this was inevitable from the moment we first met. This hunger, this driving need, is too strong to fight any more. Kiss me,' he demanded, his eyes burning into hers, his hand exerting gentle pressure so that she lowered her head and her mouth skimmed his in a tentative caress.

As she leaned over him his arms closed around her, crushing her against his chest, and his lips moved softly on hers, allowing her to set the pace and initiate her own delicate exploration. His fingers threaded through her hair, cupped her nape so that she couldn't escape even if she wanted, but she was already lost in a sea of sensation, where clinging to his shoulders was her only chance of salvation.

'I want to make love to you,' he whispered against her throat, before his mouth sought a path to the valley between her breasts and hovered there.

She felt his hand slide beneath the hem of the all-concealing nightdress, and when he drew the material up she wriggled so that he could pull it over her head. She remained kneeling on the bed while the moonlight revelled in her nakedness.

'You are exquisite,' Alex groaned as his hands cupped her pale breasts, discovered their softness and moved slowly, inexorably, towards their peaks, his thumb-pads stroking her nipples so that sensation ripped through her.

And suddenly she didn't want him to be gentle any more. He sensed her need and felt an answering shaft of desire pierce him, so that he tumbled her onto her back and came down on top of her, the tangle of sheets cast aside so that she was aware of hair-roughened thighs pressed against her skin, the throbbing hardness of his arousal pushing against her stomach. His mouth took hers with a passion that rocked her soul, and she matched him with a fervency that banished any last vestiges of doubt from his mind. She wanted him as much as he wanted her; they were drawn together by an invisible cord and there would be no going back.

Jenna whimpered low in her throat when Alex's lips

released hers to wreak havoc on her senses. He stroked his tongue across her taut nipple before taking it fully into his mouth and suckling, so that a shaft of intense pleasure unfurled in the pit of her stomach. His fingertips lightly skimmed her waist, moved lower to stroke her thighs, and then, gently but firmly, eased her legs apart to continue an erotic exploration that caused her to inhale sharply.

She wanted him, she wanted him; the litany danced in her mind, increasing in urgency as his fingers probed deeper, and she heard his husky growl of pleasure when he found her wet and so very ready for him. As he moved over her she felt a frisson of apprehension when she became aware of just how big and aroused he was, but almost instantly her fear dissipated, to be replaced with a compelling need to feel him inside her, so that they were joined as one.

He slid his hands beneath her to cup her bottom and lift her slightly, and she had no thought to deny him, but stretched her legs wider to accommodate him, unable to stifle her gasp as he entered her with one powerful stroke. For a moment she tensed—it had been a long time and her muscles were tight—but he stilled, waited, his lips moving over hers in gentle persuasion until he felt her relax, and only then did he begin to move. He set the pace, slow at first, driving into her so that the waves of pleasure built gradually, almost imperceptibly, until she found herself hovering at the edge, hardly daring to believe what was happening to her.

'Alex!' She cried his name as he thrust again, so deep and hard that she was sure she would explode with the intensity of pleasure that coursed through her. Nothing had prepared her for the exquisite sensations that her first climax brought, and she clung to him as he continued to drive into her, taking her with him when he reached the pinnacle and tumbled over.

How long they lay, replete in each other's arms, she didn't know—but when he finally stirred and eased himself out of her she was swamped by a feeling of loss and was bereft without him.

'Are you all right? I didn't hurt you?'

His voice was deep and soft, but she was beyond speech, and instead felt stupid, weak tears gather behind her eyelids and trickle down her cheek.

'My God! What have I done?'

The sight of her tears lashed his soul; he wanted to hold her, comfort her, but what comfort could he possibly offer? Because of him she had betrayed her husband—a man whom he knew hurt her and made her unhappy, yet whom she'd vowed to stay with for ever, presumably because she loved him.

'Forgive me?' he asked quietly as he rolled off the bed and pulled on his clothes. 'Although it's not you I should ask.'

Jenna was so cold her teeth chattered, and she huddled beneath the covers, not daring to look at him, although the misery and self-loathing in his voice said it all. Of course it wasn't her he needed to ask for forgiveness. It was Selina, the woman he loved and had chosen for his wife. Alex was an honourable man, he must despise himself for giving in to a momentary weakness, and he must despise her more for initiating their lovemaking.

She had practically seduced him, she thought, shuddering with shame as she recalled the way she had uncovered his body. What red-blooded male would not have responded to her blatant offer? She was entirely to blame, and as she heard him close the bedroom door behind him she buried her head in the pillows and burst into tears.

*   *   *

Alex was nowhere to be seen when she finally plucked up the courage to go downstairs, and the landlady, Mrs Pike, explained that he had gone out on the tractor with her husband to try and retrieve the car.

It was mid-morning before she heard the tractor rumble down the lane, towing the Bentley behind it, and her heart lurched in her chest as she watched Alex jump down and walk towards the pub. If she had hoped that making love with him would somehow banish her fascination for him she had been sadly mistaken; if anything she desired him even more. It was as if her body recognised its partner and was eager to rediscover the sweet pleasure only he could give.

'The car's undriveable,' he told her as he stamped his boots free of snow before following her into the bar. 'I'll arrange for a rescue truck to tow it to a garage as soon as the roads are cleared. Mr Pike has kindly agreed to lend me his Land Rover, so that I can take you to the station. You can catch a train back to London and I'll follow in a day or two, when the car's been repaired.'

Jenna nodded wordlessly, unable to look at him, and she heard him sigh heavily.

'Jenna—we need to talk.'

'Breakfast's ready,' Mrs Pike called and Jenna's stomach churned at the sight of the full English fry-up set before her. But she smiled and forced herself to tuck in; anything was better than the threatened conversation with Alex.

She remained silent on the way to the station, and he was too busy negotiating the narrow, slippery lanes to do more than throw her a concerned glance. It was only when she was standing on the platform, about to board the train, that she looked at him properly, her heart aching at his drawn, almost haggard expression.

'What are you going to say to Chris?' he asked grimly, and she frowned, guiltily recalling the web of lies she had spun. 'You don't have to stay with him. I know you believe you love him, but he has some kind of hold over you. If he really loved you he wouldn't cause you physical harm.'

His face darkened as he remembered the bruising on her foot that he had noticed the previous night, and the way she was still walking with a pronounced limp when she thought he wasn't watching her.

Alex looked desperate, Jenna admitted painfully as she climbed into a carriage and stared at the rigid set of his jaw as he waited on the platform. He obviously felt ridden with guilt that he had betrayed Selina, and believing that he had aided her in committing adultery only served to increase his self-disgust. It was time to stop the charade and give him back at least some of his self-respect.

'I do love Chris,' she said, a hurried glance along the platform revealing that the porter was still checking that the doors were safely shut. 'But he's not my husband; I was divorced three years ago.'

'Then who the hell is he?' Alex snarled, his eyes glittering as he stared past the officious porter at her.

'He's my brother,' she shouted frantically, and as she sank back in her seat she was sure that the memory of Alex's darkly furious face would be imprinted in her mind for ever.

Alex didn't return to the office for the remainder of the week, and Jenna told herself she was glad of the reprieve. There would be no escaping the conversation he had threatened when he did appear, and she resolved that there would be no more secrets between them; she would explain everything, including the existence of her daughter. He must surely despise her anyway, and the news that she was a single mother would simply be another nail in her coffin. It was time she looked for another job.

Saturday dawned cold but bright, and she took advantage of the winter sunshine to sweep up the mountain of fallen leaves in the garden, while Maisie trotted after her with her toy wheelbarrow.

This was her life now, she reminded herself as she watched her daughter run delightedly through the leaves. Her most important role was as mother to Maisie, and she wouldn't swop it for the world, but she was unable to dismiss the dull ache that settled around her heart, the feeling that she was only half alive.

She missed Alex so much it was a physical pain. If she closed her eyes she could picture his face, could see the chiselled beauty of his bone structure and the way his blue eyes glinted with amusement or darkened with pleasure when they made love. How would she ever forget him? she wondered despairingly. Even if she found a new job tomorrow and never saw him again the scent of him, the taste of him, were now an integral part of her. He was her other half. Without him she felt incomplete, but he was not hers. He loved another woman and she would have to learn to live without him.

Alex parked his car and briefly checked his appearance in the mirror, cursing to himself as he spied the cut on his chin that he had inflicted whilst shaving. As he rang the doorbell of Jenna's house he raked a hand through his hair, the betraying gesture revealing a degree of tension that was all the more irritating because it was such new territory. He was a man who liked to be in control, but where Jenna was concerned he discovered that he was as vulnerable and unsure of himself as a teenager on a first date.

He tried the bell again, stifling his impatience when it became apparent that Jenna was not at home. But as he turned to walk back down the path he heard a small voice, and glanced along the passageway that ran along the side of the house.

'You're not the milkman,' the child observed in her clear, tinkling voice, 'or the postman. Are you Father Christmas?'

For a moment he couldn't answer, shock robbing him of his power of speech as he stared down at the little girl. 'I'm afraid not,' he murmured. 'My name's Alex. Who are you?'

'Maisie Jane Deane,' she told him importantly. 'I live at sixty-three Cedar Crescent, and my rabbit's name is Smudge.'

'Maisie? Who are you talking to?' Jenna turned the corner of the house, alerted by the sound of her daughter's voice, and stopped dead. 'Alex!'

He looked horrified, there was no other way to describe his expression, and Jenna paled. 'This is my daughter, Maisie,' she explained in a faltering voice, and shrank from the glittering fury in his eyes.

'I know; we've already introduced ourselves.' He stared again at the little girl, as if he couldn't believe she was real, and then glanced at Jenna. 'Right, I'll be off, then.'

'Alex!' Shock had rooted her to the spot, but as he walked down the front path she fumbled to unlock the side gate and hurried after him. 'Alex—wait.'

The throbbing sound of his car's engine reverberated down the street and she stared after him helplessly, her heart pounding.

'So that's that,' she told Chris an hour later, after her brother had stumbled out of bed to be greeted by her tearful face. 'He took one look at Maisie and left, without giving me a chance to explain.'

'It must have been quite a shock for him, to come face to face with the daughter he never knew you had,' Chris pointed out. But Jenna wouldn't be comforted.

'You didn't see his face,' she said miserably. 'He looked at Maisie as if she was Frankenstein's daughter. For some reason he hates children. I can't carry on working for him now, but it's Christmas in a couple of weeks. What am I going to do?'

'They need someone to man the chip fryer in the burger bar,' Chris said helpfully, and she sighed. But it could come to that.

The doorbell rang, and as Chris loped off to answer it Maisie climbed up on a stool and surveyed her mother solemnly.

'Is Alex a nice man?' she queried innocently.

'No, he's an arrogant, impatient, irritating beast.'

'Thanks for the character assassination. I'm sure you can think up a few more adjectives if you try.' He appeared in the doorway, and the small kitchen immediately seemed to shrink to dolls' house size as he towered over her.

'Sneaky, stealthy,' she added to her list, but mentally admitted to gorgeous and sexy and heartbreakingly real. His presence in the kitchen was so unexpected that she had no time to muster her defences, and scrubbed her tear-stained face with the back of her hand. 'What are you doing here? I thought you had a pathological aversion to children.'

'Where ever did you get a ridiculous idea like that from?'

He seemed annoyingly calm and relaxed as he leaned against the door and folded his arms across his chest in a gesture that told her he wasn't going anywhere in a hurry.

'Margaret told me at my interview that you didn't want to appoint someone with children because of possible childcare problems. I was desperate for the job so I...'

'So you lied,' he finished for her, and she flushed.

'I didn't lie. You asked me if I was intending to produce a brood of little Deanes; you didn't ask about any existing children.'

'Jenna, have you ever heard the term splitting hairs?' He surveyed her grimly, as if she was under cross-questioning in the dock, and she discovered a sudden fascination with the floor. 'I don't dislike children. Admittedly, I haven't had much to do with them, but Maisie is—' He broke off with a shrug. 'Undoubtedly she's been beamed down from the Planet Cute. Has she inherited your temper along with your red hair?'

The warmth in his voice brought her head up, and she swallowed at the expression in his eyes, wanting nothing more than to throw herself against his chest and have him hold her.

'Maisie's much more even-tempered than me,' she admitted. 'I suppose I am quite fiery—but only when aggravated,' she added pointedly, and Alex grinned.

'I should have been warned that first day that my life would never be the same again. You fell into my arms, feisty as a she-cat, and you've proceeded to give me hell ever since.'

From the living room Jenna could hear Chris, valiantly trying to read Maisie a story. It was lunchtime, and there were things she needed to do, but she found that she was held by an invisible force, the atmosphere in the kitchen thrumming with emotions she could neither dismiss nor deny.

'You're going to marry Selina,' she stated quietly, and again Alex shook his head.

'I broke off our engagement as soon as I returned from Yorkshire.'

'Oh, no! Alex, you can't—she must have been so hurt.'

'What did you expect me to do? How could I possibly marry Selina when I was unfaithful before we even made it to the altar? She is hurt and angry, and rightly so—I've behaved appallingly—but it's my problem, Jenna, my responsibility, and nothing you can do or say will change things now.'

The note of self-loathing was back in his voice. He was a proud man, she recognised, a man with a strong sense of honour, and the fact that he had broken his own moral code filled him with shame. Perhaps he still loved Selina? If so then he must bitterly regret the one-night stand that had forced him to end his engagement, and must surely resent the fierce sexual attraction that bound him to his secretary.

'So, what happens now?' she queried huskily, her throat thick with tears that threatened to overspill. 'What happened between us was a mistake. I'm not available for casual sex whenever we happen to be working away from home.'

'Good,' he answered coolly, the warmth in his eyes belying the blandness of his tone, and she watched as he unfolded his arms and walked towards her. 'Because making love with you could never be described as casual, and I certainly can't wait until we're stranded in the back of beyond before I share your bed again.'

His arms around her were gentle but firm, drawing her inexorably closer, until his warmth, the sheer pleasure of his touch overwhelmed her and she laid her head on his chest.

'Alex, I've got Maisie, a mortgage, responsibilities,' she told him wearily, fighting the urge to wrap her arms around his waist. 'I can't just leap into an affair.'

'Can you deny that there's something between us?' he demanded fiercely, tilting her chin and brushing away an errant tear with his thumb-pad. 'Tell me you feel nothing for me, that the night we spent together was just sex, and I promise I'll leave you in peace.'

The words hovered on her tongue, but when she opened her mouth they would not come. If nothing else she owed him her honesty; she couldn't lie and tell him the most beautiful night of her life had meant nothing to her. If he walked away now he wouldn't leave her in peace, but purgatory. She needed him in the same way that she needed oxygen to breathe—but what was he offering and did she have the courage to accept?

'I wanted you from the moment you fell into my arms,' he told her as he watched the play of emotions on her face. 'Common sense dictated that you would cause havoc in my life, yet I was determined to employ you as my secretary. I can't deny that I was hoping for more than just a working relationship between us, but then you sprang the bombshell that you were married.'

Jenna had the grace to look ashamed. 'That first day in the park, you overwhelmed me. I'd never felt such a strong attraction to a man before, and I was so embarrassed. You were my boss, you'd already dismissed one secretary for being too eager, and I was desperate to save face. When I realised you thought Chris was my husband, I went along with the deception.' She stared up at him, her heart in her eyes. 'I'm sorry.'

'How sorry?' he teased gently, his fingers threading through her hair. 'Sorry enough to kiss me?'

His mouth hovered over hers, tantalisingly close yet not quite touching, and with a moan she stretched up on tiptoe to close the gap. It was like coming home after a long journey, she thought dazedly as he crushed her against his chest, the fierce possession of his lips betraying a hunger he could no longer disguise. His kiss was no gentle seduction but a passionate assault on her senses, his tongue plundering the inner sweetness of her mouth while his hands roamed her body, as if he was desperate to convince himself she was really in his arms.

'Mummy, I'm hungry.'

The small voice filtered through the haze of desire and she drew back, her eyes huge, as she was torn between her hunger for Alex and her need to answer her child's call.

There was no contest, Alex accepted—and rightly so. She would not be the woman he had come to admire if she was a half-hearted parent. For Jenna the responsibilities she felt for her small daughter ran deep. He could only hope he could convince her that there was room in her life for him.

'Alex, I…' Already she was retreating, running scared, and he dropped a light kiss on the tip of her nose as he released her.

'One day at a time, Jenna. That's all I'm asking. Discovering you have Maisie was a shock, I have to be honest—not least because although I'm sure I will like her, she may not like me, or the idea of sharing you with a man she's never met. I don't know where this is leading, sweetheart,' he admitted softly. 'If anyone had told me a couple of months ago that I would be besotted with a single mother with the uncanny knack of turning my life upside down I would have laughed. But here I am, asking for the chance to have a place in your life and Maisie's.'

'Jenna, I've put a DVD on for Maisie to watch,' Chris called from the hall. 'I'm shooting off down the pub now, with the lads. You okay?' he enquired as he stuck his head round the kitchen door and saw her standing in Alex's arms. 'I could stay if you need me?'

'I'm fine,' Jenna assured him, amused to see the way her brother and Alex were eyeing each other up. 'Alex is going to stay for lunch,' she added, glancing at him in silent query, and was rewarded with a smile that turned her legs to jelly.

She placed a couple of pizzas in the oven, made a salad and added a light dressing, all the while listening to the voices from the living room—one deep-toned, the other high-pitched and full of laughter as her daughter chattered to Alex. He had been honest when he admitted he didn't know where a relationship between them would lead, but he would not deliberately hurt Maisie, she was certain of it. She could only pray that her own emotions would remain intact.

CHAPTER EIGHT

'HAVE you ever thought about sending these to a publisher?' Alex asked as he sprawled on the sofa, flicking through the pages of the fairy stories Jenna had written and illustrated for Maisie.

'Don't look at them,' she pleaded as she finished clearing the floor of toys and reached out to take the ribbon-bound pages. 'They're just silly stories. But Maisie loves fairies, as you may have noticed,' she added with a wry smile, recalling Alex's stunned expression when he had studied the murals she had painted on her daughter's bedroom walls. 'No one else would be interested in them.'

'You have an incredible talent,' Alex said seriously, and she flushed with pleasure. 'Why did you never finish your degree?'

'Debt,' she answered bluntly. 'Lee, my ex-husband, liked to live beyond our means. When he left he took the car, the expensive stereo, and anything else that wasn't nailed down. He allowed me to keep the credit card bills he had run up in our joint names. I trusted him,' she confessed wryly. 'I was so blinded by love, or rather what I believed was love, that I went along with whatever he wanted. At the back of my mind I suppose I always knew he didn't love me—the only person Lee has ever loved is himself—but I was alone and pregnant, my parents had worries of their own, and I was just grateful that he agreed to stand by me.'

'Even so, it must have been tough,' Alex murmured, glancing at the photographs on the mantelpiece that depicted a younger-looking Jenna, a woman barely out of her teenage years, who looked swamped by the responsibility of her new baby.

'I got by,' Jenna replied, with a shrug that denounced any hint of self-pity. 'In many ways it was easier after Lee left—at least then I could control my outgoings.'

She thought back to the days when she had tried to care for Maisie while at the same time struggling to finish a poorly paid home job of wiring plugs by the hundred. In the evenings Nora had babysat, so that she could work an evening shift in a supermarket, and the memory of the mind-numbing monotony of shelf-stacking still made her shudder. Determined to create a better life for her and her daughter, she had signed up for a home study course in business and secretarial duties, and the early hours before Maisie awoke had seen her hunched over the computer, sleep deprivation a small price to pay for the chance to improve their lives.

'You should be very proud,' Alex said sincerely. 'Maisie is a beautiful little girl.'

A child who had in one day already stirred his protective instincts, he thought ruefully. In all honesty he had taken little more than a cursory interest in his sister's two boys. He enjoyed their company when he visited, and was happy in his role as uncle for a few hours, but children were an unknown entity he vaguely imagined for his future. If he hoped for any kind of relationship with Jenna he would have to accept that she would always put the welfare of her daughter before any other consideration.

'Does Lee see much of Maisie?' he asked curiously.

Jenna shrugged, her smile fading as old worries resurfaced. 'Sporadic visits every few months,' she admitted. 'He hoped for a boy—someone he could take to football—but instead Maisie was a small, colicky baby, who screamed constantly for the first three months. He once said she cramped his style, but the truth is I think we both did. The novelty of having a wife and child soon wore off, he accused me of being frigid, and to be honest sex was the last thing on my mind when I crawled into bed. It didn't take him long to seek pleasure elsewhere.'

She hesitated, compelled to confide in Alex about Lee's newfound interest in his daughter, and more importantly his plan to use Maisie as a pawn in his plan to marry his rich girlfriend. But it was too much, too soon, she decided. Alex had only just learned that she had a child. To involve him in her legal wrangles with her ex-husband would be unfair, and secretly she was afraid that he would lose interest in her. He had accused her once before of having too much baggage. Now was not the time to reveal that she had a cargo plane full.

Her ex-husband sounded an utter bastard, Alex brooded as he shifted his position on the sofa to make room for Jenna next to him. Until now he had held the opinion that couples often divorced too hastily, to the detriment of their children, but who could possibly blame Jenna for leaving a man who had been at best uninterested and at worst violent towards her? She was a devoted mother, who had sacrificed her youth and her undoubted artistic talent to care for her daughter, but the years had changed her, he realised as he glanced again at the photo of her as a young girl and compared it with the woman she was today. The innocent optimism of youth had been replaced with a determined air that was almost tangible. She was a survivor, and more than that, she was a fighter—no weak victim of her circumstances, but a woman determined to provide the best for her child. Along the way she had learned to be wary, to believe that mistrust protected her from hurt, and somehow he would have to prove that he was nothing like Lee and that she would be safe, in every sense of the word, with him.

'Are you tired now?' he asked lightly, and she shook her head, puzzled by the question.

Was he looking for a reason to leave? She had invited him to lunch and he had stayed for the rest of the day, accompanying her and Maisie to the park and taking it in his stride when the little girl had bestowed on him the honour of carrying her favourite teddy home. Maybe he had overdosed on domesticity? she thought dismally, her breath catching in her throat when he bent his head and brushed his lips over hers.

Instantly her senses clamoured for more. He had kissed her a couple of times during the afternoon, brief caresses after he had first ensured that Maisie wasn't watching, and Jenna had appreciated his sensitivity. But it hadn't allayed the almost desperate urge to have him kiss her properly. Now they were alone, and suddenly she felt ridiculously shy and unsure. It was all so frighteningly new, this sudden intimacy. She couldn't look at him without recalling the beauty of his naked body, the burning intensity in his eyes when he had come inside her.

'Why did you ask if I was tired?' she murmured, and his mouth curved into a slow, sensual smile.

'Because you're as sure as hell not frigid. I think we demonstrated that fact in Yorkshire. I asked because I thought you might need a lie-down.'

'That was very thoughtful of you,' she agreed, her eyes sparkling with humour—and something deeper.

'My motives are completely altruistic,' he assured her gravely as he lay back on the cushions and pulled her on top of him.

His jeans were old and faded, the denim stretched taut over his thighs, and as Jenna settled her weight on him she couldn't hide her shock at the hard proof of his arousal.

'Mmm, that's good,' he muttered thickly as she wriggled against him, and he moved so that their thighs were locked in an erotic simulation of lovemaking. 'You don't know how desperately I've wanted to do this all day,' he added, his hand sliding into her hair to cup her nape and draw her mouth down to his.

From the first stroke of his tongue she was on fire, and only eased away a fraction to enable him to pull her tee shirt over her head. He dispensed with her bra with similar speed and she sat astride him, her hair falling over her shoulders while his hands skimmed her ribcage to settle over each breast, his fingers moving in ever decreasing circles until they hovered over her nipples.

'Please,' she whimpered, liquid heat pooling between her thighs as he stroked each sensitive peak and then slowly drew her down so that he could repeat the action with his tongue. When at last he released her and gently pushed her up again she was trembling with need, and saw her hunger mirrored in the fierce glitter of his eyes.

'I want you,' he told her bluntly. 'Now. I can't wait.'

He swung his legs over the side of the sofa, taking her with him so that she was standing before him, and she could only watch as he wrenched open the button on her jeans, drew down the zip and tugged the material over her hips. Her knickers swiftly followed, but when she would have joined him again on the sofa he stayed her, his fingers pressing into her hips while his mouth trailed a line of fire from her navel to the junction between her thighs. Even when she guessed his intentions she couldn't quite warrant that he would do it, but as his lips moved lower and his tongue probed with gentle insistence at the entrance to her vagina she gripped his hair, at first to pull

him away and then, as pleasure overwhelmed her, to hold
him against her.

The sweet torment of his tongue took her higher and
higher; she could feel the first spasms of pleasure and
gasped. 'I want you, Alex, I want you to... Oh!'

The rest of her words were lost as a tidal wave ripped
through her, her whole body clenching and shaking so that
he had to support her legs. Only then did he draw her
down onto the sofa and stand himself, quickly dispensing
with jeans and boxers and coming down on top of her to
enter her with one powerful thrust.

Having already climaxed, Jenna's only thought was to
aid him in reaching the same heights, but as he set a
rhythm and drove into her with steady, deepening strokes
she felt the waves of pleasure build again, gradual at first,
but growing, clamouring, until she sobbed his name. She
clamped around him and he paused, fought for control,
and lost it spectacularly, his body shuddering with the
power of his release until he lay, sated and replete within
her.

'Definitely not frigid,' he teased as he smoothed her
damp hair from her face, and she smiled shyly.

'It was never like that with Lee,' she admitted huskily.
'And I've never slept with anyone else.'

'Let's keep it that way, shall we?' His voice was light
as he stood up, but there was something in his voice, a
look in his eyes, that caused her heart to thump in her
chest.

One day at a time, he had said. But the possessive
gleam in his expression told her that he wasn't just looking for a brief affair. What did he want? she wondered.
It was too soon for both of them to hope for any degree
of permanency, yet Maisie had taken an instant liking to
him. Wariness cautioned her to keep Maisie's contact with

Alex to a minimum, to protect the little girl from hurt should the affair end, but if she hoped to develop a long-term relationship with him she would have to have some faith in him.

Her stomach grumbled complainingly, and a glance at the clock revealed that it was hours since they had eaten lunch.

'Hungry?' Alex queried, and she ignored the gleam in his eyes and nodded.

'My kitchen is not the most exciting place on earth, but you're welcome to stay for dinner.'

'It's too late to cook. Do you like Chinese food? I noticed a take-away on the way here.' At her enthusiastic nod he shrugged into his jacket and dropped a brief, hard kiss on her lips. 'I won't be long—don't go away.'

Twenty minutes later Jenna smiled as she answered the phone, fully expecting to hear Alex on the line, checking her order. But the muffled voice uttering a string of expletives sent fear coiling through her.

'I'm watching you, whore. Your lover may have gone, but I'm still here.'

It had to be Lee, she reassured herself as she slammed the phone down. He had attempted to disguise his voice, but he was the only person she knew with a sick enough mind to want to scare her. Brian from across the road must have tipped Lee off about her visitor, and he was probably nowhere near, but the idea that he knew of her movements made her feel ill.

A light tap on the front door heralded Alex's return, and he frowned as he studied her pale, drawn face, and the way she folded her arms tightly across her body.

It hadn't taken long for her doubts to surface, he thought grimly. He shouldn't have left her alone even for half an hour. He should have followed his gut instinct and taken her again, made love to her until he had imprinted himself indelibly on her mind as well as her body. He was using sexual chemistry quite deliberately: the one thing he was certain of was that their passion was mutual and equal in its intensity, and if sex was the only way he could bind her to him, then for now it would have to suffice.

'I'm not hungry any more,' she informed him brightly, fighting to keep the tremor from her voice. 'I'm really sorry, but I'm exhausted—you've worn me out. If you don't mind, I'd really like to go to bed. On my own.'

The last was on a note of sheer panic and Alex studied her quietly. 'What's the matter?'

'Nothing.'

The phone rang, its strident peal making her jump like a startled doe, but as she reached to answer it he plucked the receiver from her fingers. He waited impassively until the string of foul insults came to an end and then spoke, his voice dangerously calm, hiding the fact that he was ready to commit murder.

'Presumably you're unaware that this line is being monitored by the phone company,' he lied, 'and that your call has been recorded? As Jenna's barrister, I look forward to seeing you in court.' He had been unable to stop the fury in his voice; it was a miracle he had restrained himself at all, and his face darkened as he stared at Jenna. 'That wasn't the first malicious call you've received— don't even try to deny it. Do you have any idea who's behind them? Lee?' he suggested, when she remained silent.

'I don't know… Yes, I would guess Lee. The voice is muffled, but there's no one else that warped. But, Alex, you've made things worse. I know you're trying to help, but now he'll be angry—' She broke off, her face tight with fear and misery.

'First thing tomorrow I'll call the phone company and have your number changed to an ex-directory one. Then I'll inform the police that you're being hounded. Sweetheart, there are laws to prevent jerks like your ex-husband from frightening you,' he continued, but she shook her head, her eyes wide with panic.

'You don't understand. Lee's clever. He'd probably tell the police that I'm mad, and a bad mother to Maisie. He'd do anything to take her away from me.'

'Are you saying that he wants custody of Maisie? I thought he wasn't interested in her?'

'He wasn't until a few weeks ago.' Realising that Alex wouldn't rest until he had dragged the whole story from her, she explained about Lee's wealthy girlfriend and the reason behind his renewed interest in his daughter.

'He really doesn't stand a chance of winning sole custody,' Alex sought to reassure her, after persuading her to eat some dinner. 'Call his bluff. Let the courts decide. I have friends who specialise in family law; I can ensure that you're represented by the best lawyers.'

Perhaps Alex was right, Jenna thought wearily as she went upstairs to bed. She had eventually persuaded him to return to his flat for the night, assuring him that she would be fine and that Chris would soon be home. Alex had made it plain that he would be happier spending the night, even promising to sleep on the sofa, but she was desperate not to rush their relationship. She didn't want Maisie to wake up and find him at the breakfast table; it was too soon.

The phone rang, and she let it ring and ring until she could bear it no longer. But when she snatched up the receiver it was Chris at the other end of the line.

'I'm in the pub,' he said, his voice barely audible above

the background hum. 'We're going on to a club and I'll stay over at Nick's tonight. Will you be okay?'

'Of course,' she told him firmly. 'I lived on my own for three years. Have a good time.'

No way was she going to spoil Chris's evening, she decided as she fell into bed. Alex was right. Lee couldn't hurt her, and his chances of gaining custody of Maisie were remote. For some reason she had allowed him to frighten her, as he had done during their marriage, but she was no longer a timid young girl, struggling with the demands of a new baby, she was an independent woman and she could stand up to Lee.

She slept surprisingly well, and woke just as it was getting light, a small sound from outside her bedroom door warning her that Maisie must be awake.

'Maisie!' Usually the little girl liked to snuggle down in her bed for an early-morning cuddle, and she frowned when there was no reply.

The sound came again, and she recognised it as the loose floorboard at the top of the stairs. Her heartbeat slowed again as she berated herself for being over-imaginative. It must be Chris trying to creep up to bed without waking her, she decided, and she knotted the belt of her robe around her waist and opened her bedroom door—her scream echoing throughout the house as she came face to face with her ex-husband.

'You frightened me, Lee. What are you doing here? How did you get in?' She was shaking so hard that she had to lean against the wall, acute shock making her feel so sick that her brow was clammy with beads of sweat.

'That lock on the back door was never very secure. I used to live here, remember?'

'What do you want?'

'To talk to you. But maybe you've got company?' His sly smile infuriated her, and she stood away from the wall.

'Well, I haven't. I'm here on my own, apart from Maisie. Not that it's any of your business,' she added, as she checked on her daughter and found her still asleep. 'You'd better go downstairs. I'm surprised Maisie hasn't been disturbed already. You have no right to break into my house,' she told him as she slammed about the kitchen, the familiarity of filling the kettle and making tea giving her a measure of control over the situation. 'What's so urgent that you had to talk to me at eight o'clock on a Sunday morning?' She knew why he was here, of course; he had hoped to catch her with her lover. But his words stunned her.

'I want Maisie for Christmas.'

'Gift wrapped?' she queried sarcastically, and his face tightened.

'Don't get clever with me. Louise is planning a big Christmas celebration. Her parents are coming for dinner, and she thought it would be a good time for them to meet Maisie. They're going to be her new grandparents after all.'

'Maisie isn't even four years old yet. She's too young to spend Christmas away from home,' Jenna argued.

'When I win custody the Love Nest *will* be her home.'

Jenna's brows shot up. 'The Love Nest?' she repeated faintly.

'It's Louise's house—my house, after we're married. Louise has got it all planned. She's bought loads of presents for Maisie, and she wants to dress her up and—'

'Stick her on top of the Christmas tree?' Jenna finished for him furiously.

'So you're refusing to allow me to spend Christmas with my daughter? That's not going to look good in court.

I'm trying to come to an amicable arrangement—but then you always were a bit unbalanced.'

'How dare you?' Jenna glared at him wildly, but then took a deep breath; she was playing straight into Lee's hands. 'All right, Maisie can spend Christmas Day with you. But you bring her back on Boxing Day. After that we'll go to court and see if we can come to a fair arrangement over access.'

Lee gave a satisfied smile. 'Great, Louise has other arrangements for Boxing Day anyway. Here, let me do that.' He took the kettle from her and poured boiling water into the teapot—and then over her hand.

'Lee, watch what you're doing—you've burned me.' Jenna thrust her hand under the cold tap, blinking back tears as her skin began to blister.

'Sorry, my hand slipped.'

'Rubbish! You did that on purpose, you bastard. How can I possibly let Maisie go with you?'

'Don't you worry. I'll treat her with kid gloves,' Lee promised cheerfully, and for once she believed him. Lee needed Maisie; he wouldn't do anything that would jeopardise his chances with his girlfriend, which meant he had to prove that he was a perfect father.

Alex phoned mid-morning, and at the sound of his deep, familiar voice Jenna sat at the bottom of the stairs and tried to disguise the fact that she was crying.

'I thought we could go out for lunch—somewhere they cater for children, obviously. I'll be over in an hour.'

'No!' Jenna stopped him with a frantic cry.

She needed to spend some time alone, to get a grip on herself after Lee's visit and hide the evidence that he had hurt her in another so-called accident. He had done it to scare her, of course, to show her that she was still under his control. Part of her wanted to fight him, report him to the police for assault and see him prosecuted. But what if no one believed her story? What if Lee managed to convince the courts that she was paranoid and an unsuitable mother?

She was so tempted to confide in Alex. She trusted him implicitly, and knew she could depend on him—but that was the trouble. She didn't want to go into another relationship where she was the needy one. Her relationship with Alex was already unbalanced; he was a wealthy, successful and highly eligible bachelor and she was a financially challenged single mother. Pride dictated that she sort out her problems with Lee by herself.

'Maisie's unwell today,' she lied. 'I want her to have a quiet day at home. I'll see you tomorrow.'

'She seemed fine yesterday,' Alex pointed out, although in fairness he had to admit that his knowledge of a small child's health was limited.

'Well, she's not today.' Jenna cut the call before it became an argument and paced the house, her nerves so on edge that eventually she bundled Maisie into her coat and took her for a walk.

Alex was leaning against the bonnet of his car when they returned from the park, and despite everything Jenna felt the familiar butterflies in the pit of her stomach. Why did he have to be so gorgeous? she thought despairingly as he watched her approach, the expression in his eyes unfathomable. His jeans, sweater and leather jacket were black, the uniform colour emphasising his height and the width of his shoulders. She couldn't drag her eyes from his face, and as her gaze hovered on his mouth she recalled with stark clarity the way it had felt on her body, when his tongue had brought her to the edge of ecstasy and pushed her over.

'Are you feeling better, poppet?' Alex asked Maisie

gently, hunkering down in front of her so that his face was on a level with hers.

Maisie scrambled off her bike, her face beaming. 'Alex, have you come to play with me?'

'Absolutely—if that's okay with Mummy?' His eyes travelled over Jenna, noting her pallor and the flare of panic she hadn't been able to disguise when she had first seen him.

Silently she opened the front door and stepped aside to usher him in, but as she slipped out of her jacket he caught sight of the blister on her hand.

'It's nothing,' she assured him, hastily tugging her sleeve down to try and hide the angry red mark, but Alex ignored her and took her hand in both of his to inspect it. 'I spilt some boiling water while I was making the tea this morning,' she explained huskily, her gaze skittering away under the steady watchfulness of his.

'Lee was here, wasn't he?'

'How do you know that?'

'You've just told me,' he said gently. 'Why did you let him in?'

The silence lasted for several minutes before Jenna finally admitted, 'He broke in early this morning. I think he was checking up on me. He seemed to think someone—you—had stayed the night.'

'I wish to blazes I had,' Alex bit out, trying to rein in his anger. Jenna had suffered enough, he thought grimly, glancing again at her blistered hand. He would find an outlet for his fury later—preferably with his fist and her damn ex-husband's face. 'Where's your brother?'

'Chris stayed at a friend's last night. He phoned just after you left. I had no reason to think Lee would come here,' Jenna whispered. 'He wanted to persuade me to allow Maisie to spend Christmas Day with him and his girlfriend.'

'And his form of persuasion was to hurt you?' Alex ground out.

'He said it was an accident,' Jenna replied quietly, 'but I don't think it was. I've agreed, reluctantly, to let Maisie go to him for Christmas, but in the New Year I'll have to let the courts decide on her future.' The thought brought fresh tears to her eyes, and as Alex groaned and put his arms around her she lay weakly against his chest, absorbing his strength.

'Darling, it'll be okay. I promise you.' His mouth moved across her hair, kissed away her tears, and settled on her lips in a sweetly evocative caress that offered comfort rather than passion.

Jenna refused point-blank to go to the casualty unit, and, realising that her composure was paper-thin, he had to content himself with tending to her injured hand himself, covering the burn with a sterile dressing from the medical box. The rest of the day passed quietly, and he devoted his attention to entertaining Maisie, who was fast taking up a special place in his heart.

'Maisie likes you,' Jenna admitted that evening as he made to leave.

He had been adamant at first that he wouldn't allow her to remain in the house, and had suggested that she and Maisie move into his flat. Imagining his elegant apartment, which overlooked the Thames, Jenna had panicked at the thought of filling it with Maisie's toys, and had hastily pointed out that her daughter needed to be near her nursery.

Unconvinced, Alex had spoken at length to Chris, who had assured him he would never leave Jenna alone at night again, and the two of them had checked the window locks and repaired the bolt on the back door.

'Does Maisie liking me bother you?' he asked softly, and Jenna bit her lip.

'I just don't want her to be hurt, that's all. If this ends—us, I mean; our affair—I don't want her to suffer.' She heard Alex sigh as he drew her against his chest, his hand winding into her hair so that he could tilt her face up to his.

'I've given you my word that I would never knowingly hurt you or Maisie, but you'll have to put some faith in me. Without trust on both sides, any relationship between us is doomed.'

He kissed her then, with a fierce passion that shook her, and suddenly there was nothing but Alex and the seductive stroke of his tongue, his eyes glittering with unspoken desire when at last he set her free.

'You can't deny this, Jenna, any more than I can. I've never wanted any woman the way I want you. You're in my blood, coursing through my veins. I can't think straight when you're around, and when you're not I can't think at all because I miss you so much. Give me a chance, sweetheart, please. Don't let your ex-husband ruin what we have.'

Alex was right, Jenna admitted as she stared down at her small daughter's sleeping form before she went to bed. She couldn't spend the rest of her life in fear of Lee.

She believed Alex when he said that he would never knowingly hurt her, but he was unaware of how important he was to her. In a few months he might decide their affair had run its course, and he would undoubtedly suggest that for Maisie's sake they remain friends. It would be the sensible, civilised thing to do, but she didn't feel sensible where Alex was concerned. Her emotions were all over the place. And she wasn't sure she was brave enough to risk her heart again.

CHAPTER NINE

THE woman in the mirror looked like a drab sparrow, Jenna thought disgustedly. She had donned her old grey suit, the colour matching her mood, her hair was scraped back into a severe ponytail, and without a scrap of make-up her face appeared pinched and wan. There was a defeated air about her, as if she had already conceded victory to Lee, and suddenly she was filled with a burning anger.

Once before she had allowed him to browbeat her and manipulate her, but then she had been a girl barely out of her teens, her world turned upside down by the demands of a new baby. Lee had played on her inexperience, chipping away at her confidence, and the harder she had tried to please him the less she had seemed able to do anything right in his eyes.

It was only after he had left and her parents had sent her the money to fly to New Zealand to visit them that the extent of the damage he had inflicted had become apparent. Her family had been shocked to see how their once vibrant, happy daughter had become so timid and withdrawn, and had done their best to persuade her to stay permanently in New Zealand.

It had been tempting, Jenna recalled. She'd had so little faith in herself at that point that she could easily have taken up her parents' offer to care for Maisie while she sorted her life out, but the holiday, the time away from Lee, had given her a chance to think straight, and some of the old Jenna returned. She had brought Maisie back to England and set about changing their lives. Along the way her confidence and sense of self-worth had returned—so why was she allowing Lee to destroy her for the second time? she berated herself.

She was worth a thousand Lees, she told her reflection as she changed into the cream suit Alex had bought her. She was a far better parent than Lee could ever be, and although she respected his right for fair access to his daughter, he would not intimidate her again. With a renewed sense of determination she emphasised the colour of her eyes with a soft grey eyeshadow, added blusher and lipgloss, and combed her hair loose.

Her confidence jumped several notches at the admiring glances she received when she strode into the office block.

Alex was standing in the reception area, chatting with members of his legal team, but he looked up as she stepped out of the lift and she saw him stiffen, his eyes locked on her, while a stain of dark colour ran the length of his cheekbones. For several minutes he was unable to disguise the effect she had on him, and he murmured a distracted comment to his companion as she strolled past, her smile brief and impersonal, hiding her surge of delight at the proof that he did genuinely desire her.

She was determined that their relationship would not become common knowledge among the other members of staff. There would be no overt flirting, no snatched kisses in the stationery cupboard—but it was cheering to discover that he would be suffering as much as she.

It was a busy morning; Alex was tied up with appointments with clients, and in his free moments had to deal with several urgent phone calls. When Jenna took in his coffee she sensed his growing impatience.

'I've hardly seen you all morning,' he complained. 'How are you today? Is your hand healing?'

'It's fine,' she assured him. 'I'm fine. I don't know what

happened to me at the weekend. I'm not usually so pathetic. I'm determined not to let Lee bother me.'

'You're not pathetic,' Alex told her gruffly. 'You were terrified by your ex-husband—anyone would have been upset. But I'm glad you're feeling more positive. You look stunning,' he added. 'I'm not sure how long I can last in keeping our relationship a secret. You don't know how tempted I am to rip your clothes off, lean you across my desk and take you.'

'Alex!' Jenna instantly lost all sense of composure, her face flaming, and he chuckled unrepentantly.

'It's hell, isn't it? I'm seriously thinking of installing a shower in my office, with just the cold tap plumbed in.'

'I think I'd better get back to work,' she muttered hastily, and his face became more serious.

'I'm busy at lunchtime, but I'll drive you home tonight, okay?'

She felt a stab of panic that Lee's lookout, Brian, would be watching, and then gave herself a mental shake. 'That would be nice; stay for dinner.'

She went to lunch alone, as Margaret had taken the day off. Alex's personal assistant was so much happier as a result of his organising nursing care for her husband, and Jenna smiled as she joined the queue in the self-service restaurant; it was hard to believe that she had once thought Alex to be hard and unfeeling!

'Let me take that,' said a voice from above her head, and she glanced round, startled to find Selina Carter-Lloyd next to her. 'There's a space on my table over in the corner, if you'd like to join me.'

Selina commandeered the tray and paid for the meal before Jenna could remonstrate, and she had little option but to follow her to a secluded part of the restaurant.

'There was no need for you to pay for my lunch,' she

stated firmly, pulling out her purse to reimburse the other woman.

'I want to talk to you,' Selina said determinedly, and Jenna sighed.

'Yes, I gathered that. What about?' she enquired coolly, although there could only be one subject that Selina wished to discuss with her.

'Alex is making the biggest mistake of his life, and it's all your fault.' Selina launched into her attack. 'He loves me. He always has. A marriage between us has been on the cards for years, but I was happy to wait until Alex had built up his career. My parents own swathes of Hampshire,' Selina continued haughtily, 'and I'm their only child; everything will eventually pass to me and my future husband—Alex. It's all planned, and I won't let him throw away our future because of a stupid obsession with his secretary.'

Jenna took a deep breath. 'I understand how hurt you must be, but I've never put any pressure on Alex—far from it. Alex chose to end his engagement to you.'

'Only because he feels sorry for you,' Selina snapped. 'He explained that he felt guilty, because he seduced you and then discovered you were a struggling single mother. He felt he had no option but to stand by you.'

Jenna swallowed and put down her fork, her meal untouched. She suddenly felt very sick as doubts surged through her. How did Selina know so much about her situation? Alex had to have told her. She had always felt that he regretted ending his relationship with Selina, and had done so through a sense of honour because he had been unfaithful to her. Could it be true? she wondered bleakly. Could he still be in love with Selina and only continuing his affair with herself out of guilt?

'He stands to lose so much,' Selina pushed on, seeing

the doubts in Jenna's eyes. 'And if he knew about the baby…'

'Are you telling me you're pregnant with Alex's child?' Jenna asked huskily. There was a long pause.

'I lost the baby,' Selina eventually admitted. 'It was early days. Alex never knew, and I felt I couldn't say anything after he broke off our engagement.'

'I'm sorry; I think you should tell him about the baby, and how you feel, and let him decide if he really does want to marry you after all. I certainly wouldn't stand in his way.'

'Unfortunately at the moment he's besotted with you,' Selina snorted impatiently. 'Who can underestimate the power of sex? If you were no longer around his fascination with you would soon fade, and to that end I'm prepared to be extremely generous.'

Jenna stared at the open chequebook and her eyes widened. 'Are you offering to pay me off?'

'I know that your finances are somewhat…straitened,' Selina said coolly. 'I'll give you one year's salary if you leave Morrell and Partners by the end of the week. That'll tide you over until you find another job—preferably on the other side of the world.'

Jenna stood up, her movements carefully controlled as she fought to keep a lid on her temper. 'Thank you for the offer, Miss Carter-Lloyd, but I'm afraid I must refuse. Surely you can't want Alex if the only way you can get him to marry you is to bribe the opposition?'

'You're making a big mistake,' Selina hissed furiously, her cheeks flushed with angry colour. 'Alex will see the error of his ways eventually. You'll run out of tricks to keep him entertained and he'll start thinking with his head again, instead of his trousers!'

Her venomous words ran round and round in Jenna's

head as she walked back to the office, and it came as a
relief to discover that Alex was in a meeting and would
be unavailable for most of the afternoon. She couldn't
face him right now, Jenna thought numbly as she tried to
concentrate on her work. He knew her so well he would
recognise instantly that something was troubling her, and,
being Alex, wouldn't rest until he had dragged the truth
from her.

It was almost five o'clock and she was packing up her
work when he came into her office, his heavy frown warning her that he was not in the best of moods.

'Something's come up,' he said without preamble. 'I
can't take you home tonight.'

'That's all right. Some other time, perhaps,' she murmured, but her answer barely seemed to register, and he
disappeared back into his own office with a distracted air.

It was bitterly cold and wet when she stepped out of
the office block, and the gaudy brilliance of the Christmas
lights seemed to emphasise the gloomy night as she joined
the throng of commuters streaming towards the underground station. Christmas was just over a week away, but
Jenna had lost all enthusiasm for it, knowing that Maisie
would be spending the day with Lee. For her daughter's
sake she would have to try and dredge up some festive
spirit—Maisie was already wildly excited, and tonight she
had promised that they would decorate the enormous
Christmas tree that Chris had only managed to squeeze
into the living room after he had lopped six inches off the
top.

As she crossed the road a car splashed through a puddle, the wheels throwing a spray of muddy water up the
backs of her legs, and she turned to glare at the driver,
her heart stopping for several seconds as she recognised
Alex, sitting in the back of the Bentley with Selina Carter-

Lloyd beside him. The two of them appeared to be deep in conversation, and Jenna shot down the steps leading to the underground station as if the hounds of hell were behind her.

So Selina was the 'something' that had cropped up, she surmised bleakly. Would she tell Alex that she had miscarried his child? she wondered. Selina was desperate to win Alex back, and her offer of a bribe to keep Jenna away from him had been hugely insulting, but at the same time her words had been undeniably true. Selina came from Alex's world. She would make him an ideal wife, and could offer him wealth and, from the sound of it, half of Hampshire. By contrast, all Jenna could offer was a pre-school child, an ex-husband, and the prospect of a bitter legal battle. She didn't need a financial reward to end her relationship with Alex; for his sake it was simply the right thing to do.

The next day she determined to keep out of Alex's way as much as possible, but mid-morning he called her into his office, and her heart sank as he requested she close the door behind her.

'There's something I want to talk to you about,' he informed her as he swung away from the window, but when she dared to glance at him she found that he was smiling and relaxed.

'I need to talk to you too,' she replied quietly, and at her tone he gave her a long, assessing stare.

'You first.'

Jenna took a deep breath. 'I saw you and Selina together last night.'

'I gave her a lift,' Alex admitted. 'But from your voice I suspect that you've put two and two together and made at least fifteen.'

'Did she tell you that we had lunch together yesterday?

Her choice, not mine,' she added dryly, as Alex frowned. 'She told me, among other things, that she had recently miscarried your baby.'

Jenna didn't know what she had expected Alex's re-action to be, but his harsh shout of laughter shocked her.

'Well, it was the immaculate bloody conception. Selina and I have never been lovers,' he said forcefully, and Jenna shook her head in confusion.

'But you were engaged.'

'I knew it was a mistake from the minute I asked her to marry me,' he admitted quietly as he moved away from her to stare out of the window again. 'Discovering that I was physically unable to make love to her rather em-phasised the point. If Selina was pregnant, which I very much doubt, it wasn't my child she was carrying.'

The resoluteness of his tone brooked no further argu-ment, but Jenna still murmured faintly, 'She was very con-vincing. I'd rather you were honest with me.'

'I am being honest, damn it!' He rounded on her, his eyes flashing with fury, and Jenna felt her own temper rise.

'Why would she lie?'

'To cause trouble between us, I imagine. If that was her aim, it seems she's been successful.'

Jenna bit her lip, torn by her desire to believe him and the stark reality that he would be better off with Selina. 'She said a lot of other things…'

'I bet she did.' He took his hands out of his pockets and forced himself to relax as he crossed the room and pulled her into his arms. 'I hurt her, badly, and I'm not proud of that. But I don't want to marry her. I want you.'

Alex's desire for her was not in question, Jenna thought bleakly as he drew her against his chest, his hand soothing her as he stroked her hair. And standing in his arms like this she could almost kid herself that she was content, but a relationship built on sexual attraction was bound to falter; her marriage to Lee had proved that. She wanted more than just his body—although, God forgive her, that was enough to risk her heart and happiness for—but she loved him enough to want what was right for him, and she suspected that one day he would realise that Selina was that person.

'What did you want to talk to me about?' she asked, forcing herself to draw out of his arms, and he sighed.

'I've received some reports on Lee,' he told her; moving to sit behind his desk and indicating that she should take a seat.

'What kind of reports?' Jenna enquired with a puzzled frown, and he sat back and subjected her to a long stare.

'I employed a private detective to run some checks on your ex. He's come back with some interesting facts—the most pertinent being that Lee owes at least fifty thousand pounds to various credit card and loan companies.'

'How can your detective possibly have found that out?' Jenna gasped, her mind reeling. 'Surely that kind of information is confidential?'

'You can find out pretty well anything if you're prepared to pay for the information,' Alex told her bluntly, and once again she recognised the ruthless streak that hid behind his charm. 'Were you aware of Lee's debts?'

'Of course not. But I'm not surprised—he always liked the finer things in life. What about his girlfriend? Do you think she knows how much trouble he's in?'

'I'm not sure,' Alex admitted quietly. 'Louise Henry appears to be an astute businesswoman. The dating agency she runs is extremely successful, and she's built up an extensive property portfolio. She's either blinded by Lee's charms, or—as I suspect is more likely—she is aware of his financial problems and is using that knowledge as leverage.'

'Leverage for what?' Jenna muttered in confusion.

Alex hesitated for a moment and then continued. 'Miss Henry has been married twice before, but neither relationship produced any children. My informant got chatting with some of her friends at the gym, and I don't think you should underestimate her desperation for a child. It's possible that she's agreed to clear Lee's debts if in return he'll marry her and provide her with the child she longs for: Maisie.'

Jenna had harboured similar suspicions herself, but had berated herself for being over-imaginative. To hear Alex voice her worst fears made her feel ill. 'In effect, she's trying to buy my daughter,' she whispered miserably.

'Presumably it all hinges on Lee winning full custody of Maisie; I can't think of any other reason why she'd want to marry him.'

'Which is why Lee is so determined to prove that I'm an unsuitable mother,' Jenna surmised. 'I would never prevent Lee from seeing Maisie, but she's my baby. I've brought her up virtually single-handed for the last three years. He can't possibly win, can he?'

'It seems unlikely,' Alex agreed. 'But I can't give you a one hundred per cent guarantee that the courts won't decide in his favour. I imagine Lee and Louise will promote themselves as a devoted, happy couple who can offer Maisie a stable home life.'

'Are you suggesting that I don't already do that?' Jenna snapped, and he held up his hand placatingly.

'You work full-time; Maisie spends most of her days in a nursery or being cared for by your elderly neighbours. I know the truth, that you're an exemplary mother, but it's not me you'll have to convince. It's the judge.'

'Oh, God!' Jenna twisted her fingers together in anguish and Alex pressed home his advantage.

'I have a suggestion,' he stated coolly as he scraped back his chair and walked back over to the window, so that his back was to her. 'I think we should get married.'

For a moment the room seemed to sway alarmingly, and Jenna had to force air into her lungs. 'Do you mean to each other?' she managed, wondering if he was playing some sort of cruel joke.

'Of course to each other,' he snapped sarcastically. 'Unless you've someone else lined up?'

'I don't have anyone lined up. Getting married isn't high on my list of priorities—although I can see that for me it would certainly be beneficial to have a wealthy husband and a proper home for Maisie.'

'Naturally you would be able to give up work and concentrate on being a full-time mother.' Alex dangled the bait cleverly, and she had to bite her lip to prevent herself from throwing caution to the wind and accepting his incredible offer.

'But what would you get out of it?'

'You in my bed on a permanent basis,' he stated bluntly, and the tiny flame of hope that had flickered in her chest since he'd first voiced his suggestion was quickly extinguished.

'Sex isn't a proper basis for marriage,' she said huskily. 'Even good sex.'

She recalled Selina's statement that Alex was obsessed with her. Sexual desire was a potent force that overruled common sense, as she had found out when she married Lee. Alex might desire her now, she could even believe that he cared for her—and Maisie, in his way—but he had never mentioned love. It was tempting to accept his offer, if for no other reason than to secure Maisie's future, but she couldn't bear to watch as Alex's passion for her faded, leaving nothing in its place.

'You must see that it would never work,' she murmured. 'You need a wife who can share the demands of your career, who can host dinner parties and entertain your clients. If you married me you'd probably live on fish fingers,' she quipped, trying to hide the fact that she was breaking up inside.

'I don't want you for your culinary expertise,' Alex growled, so fiercely that she was forced to believe him. It was her expertise in the bedroom he was interested in, she conceded, although even that was debatable.

'A marriage between us wouldn't work because we don't love each other,' Jenna stated firmly. 'I already have one disastrous attempt behind me, yet at the time I truly believed that I loved Lee and he loved me. I'm not sure I'll ever trust my judgement enough to make such a commitment again, and I'm certainly not going to get married for the sake of convenience.'

Alex was silent for so long that she could only hazard a guess at his thoughts while he stood, his shoulders rigid, staring out over the city.

'I can see I'll have to find the thumbscrews,' he said lightly, turning to face her at last, the expression in his dark eyes unfathomable, although the smile he gave seemed genuine enough.

Was there a hint of relief about him? she wondered painfully. Perhaps he had only asked her to marry him out of a sense of duty, a concern for Maisie? He had said he wanted her in his bed, but in all honesty there were any number of willing volunteers eager to fill the post of his lover, and she would bet that none of them had a child in tow.

'What happens between us now?' she asked quietly, sure that he would want to end their relationship.

'Nothing,' he replied, with a shrug that spoke of indifference and hid his inner frustration.

He had rushed her, and if he didn't tread carefully he would lose her completely. He had underestimated the damage her damned ex-husband had inflicted on her self-esteem, the devastation Lee had wrought on her ability to trust her own emotions. He had lost serious ground, Alex conceded bitterly, but he wouldn't lose her—not without a fight.

'I don't see why we can't carry on as we were. You still want me as much as I want you,' he added, with a flash of his old arrogance, and despite everything she found she was powerless to resist his kiss, her arms moving of their own accord to wind around his neck as the pressure of his mouth increased.

Feeling her willing response, he tightened his arms around her, one hand sliding down to cup her bottom and pull her hard against his thighs so that she was made achingly aware of his hunger. When he finally released her she was flushed and trembling, shamingly aware that if he repeated his suggestion to make love to her across his desk she would willingly comply.

'This hasn't changed,' he told her softly, 'and nothing Lee or Selina can do or say will alter my desire for you.'

He insisted on driving her home after work, stopping off on the way to collect Maisie. The nursery had held a Christmas party, and Maisie skipped out to the car looking utterly adorable in her fairy costume, complete with wings, which Jenna had constructed from wire coat hangers and net curtains.

'I look like a real fairy, don't I?' the little girl demanded, and Alex felt a gentle tug on his heart as he lifted her into the car and fastened her safety harness.

If anyone had told him six months ago that he would be seriously considering exchanging his bachelor lifestyle for fatherhood he would have laughed, he admitted with a rueful smile. He had assured Jenna that he would never upset her or her daughter, and the truth was that doing so would be akin to cutting his heart out.

'You certainly do,' he assured Maisie gravely as he struggled to accommodate her wings beneath the child restraint, and, watching them, Jenna felt a pang of dismay.

It was plain that Maisie adored Alex, and he seemed to be genuinely fond of her. Maybe she should have accepted his marriage proposal and prayed for a miracle, she fretted. Perhaps in time Alex would have grown to love her. But it was too late now. She could hardly tell him she had changed her mind.

He stayed for dinner, and as Jenna tucked Maisie into bed the butterflies in the pit of her stomach set up a clog dance, her nerves stretched to breaking point when she went back downstairs. Would he expect to stay the night? she wondered, the sight of him sprawled on the sofa setting up a slow, steady drumbeat of desire in her veins. He had discarded his tie and unbuttoned the top couple of buttons of his shirt so that she could glimpse the dark hairs that covered his chest. His body was lean and hard, so sexy that she felt a shiver run the length of her spine, and her face flamed when he glanced up and saw the unguarded expression in her eyes.

'Come here,' he commanded, and she gave up any semblance of trying to act cool and fell into his arms. 'My parents have invited us to spend Christmas Day with them,' he murmured long moments later, as she balanced on his knee, her mouth swollen from the fierce hunger of his, her blouse and bra lying in a pile at her feet. 'I accepted on your behalf.'

'Alex, I don't think…' In truth she could barely concentrate on his words; she simply wanted him to continue his sweet sorcery, her breasts aching for his possession, and she frowned as he reached for her blouse and slid it over her shoulders. 'I'm not sure that's a good idea. Your parents must have been hoping that Selina would accompany you. What will they think of me?'

He caught the note of uncertainty in her voice and stared at her with quiet determination. 'They're looking forward to meeting you. They're quite aware that I intend to spend Christmas Day with you, so either we both visit them or we don't. It's your choice.'

'That's not fair,' Jenna muttered distractedly, unable to hide her dismay as he fastened the buttons of her blouse. Perhaps his much-vaunted desire for her was fading already.

'How were you planning to spend Christmas Day, then? Other than moping around missing Maisie and feeling sorry for yourself?' He ignored her furious gasp and continued, 'Chris has been invited to spend Christmas with his new girlfriend's family, but he's refused on the grounds that he felt he should stay with you.'

'I don't want him to do that,' Jenna muttered miserably, and was rewarded with a smile.

'Good! Tell him you're going to spend the day with me and he can go off and enjoy himself without feeling guilty.' He eased her off his lap and stood up, reaching for his jacket.

'You don't have to go just yet,' Jenna murmured, aware that she was blushing as she cast pride aside and made it plain that she hoped he would stay. He gave her a gentle smile.

'Yes, I do. Don't get me wrong. I want to make love to you quite desperately. But, as you said earlier, sex isn't a proper basis for a relationship. I need to know exactly what you want from me, and I'm not sure you even know that yourself yet. But I can wait. I want to prove that there is more than just physical desire between us, and to do that sex needs to go on the back burner for a while.'

He'd picked a fine time to be honourable, Jenna thought irritably as she tossed beneath the sheets later that night, her body burning up with sexual frustration that made sleep impossible. She loved him, but right now she hated him too—hated the ease with which he could arouse her senses to fever-pitch and then just walk away, spouting some nonsense about a platonic relationship.

She vented her frustration on her unsuspecting pillow until it was pummelled into submission and eventually fell asleep, unaware that across town Alex was taking a long, cold shower.

CHAPTER TEN

THE LOVE NEST was a mock-Georgian house at the end of a sweeping drive, and Jenna viewed the marble pillars and the stone lions that guarded the front steps with dismay.

'I wonder if Louise Henry has ever heard the expression, ''less is more'',' Alex murmured, and she bit back a smile.

'It looks very nice,' Jenna lied, turning to Maisie and determinedly blinking back her tears. 'There's Daddy and Auntie Louise, darling. You're going to have a wonderful time with them, and Father Christmas is going to make a special trip to leave your presents under the tree when you come home.'

Maisie looked unconvinced, but went to Lee quite readily, and Jenna told herself she was glad—she wanted Maisie to have a good relationship with her father.

Louise Henry looked slightly older than she had imagined. She seemed rather shy and gentle, not the hard-nosed businesswoman Jenna had pictured, and for Maisie's sake she was glad. Lee might not win full custody of their daughter, but if they came to an arrangement of shared care then Louise would be an important person in Maisie's life, and it would be necessary to put any feelings of jealousy aside and try to get on.

'She'll be fine,' Alex assured her softly as they drove away, and Jenna nodded.

'I know, Louise actually seems quite nice. But it's Christmas Eve, and Maisie should be at home hanging up her stocking.' She swallowed hard and stared unseeingly out of the window as the car sped along the motorway.

Alex's parents lived in a tiny village in Kent, and as he swung through the gates leading to their house she dredged up a smile, determined not to spoil Christmas for everyone else.

She need not have been so worried about meeting Alex's parents, she mused later that night as she prepared for bed. Katharine and Lionel Morrell could not have been more welcoming, and any fears Jenna had harboured that they would be disappointed Alex had brought her rather than Selina had quickly been dispelled. It had been a lovely evening, she thought as she slid into her bed in the pretty guest room she had been allocated.

'My room's next door,' Alex had informed her, and as she snuggled under the duvet she forced her mind to dwell on anything but the image of him getting undressed on the other side of the wall.

Lucky him to be able to put passion 'on the back burner', as he had so poetically put it, while she seemed to be a cauldron of seething emotions that were in danger of boiling over. He had accused her of not knowing what she wanted from him, but she knew only too well. She wanted his heart as well as his body; she wanted his eyes to light up every time he looked at her, his stern face to soften. Put bluntly, she wanted him to love her as she loved him. But he seemed as out of her reach as he had done the first day she had fallen into his arms.

Then she had considered him to be urbane, sophisticated and way out of her league, and now, meeting his parents, being a guest at their elegant Christmas Eve dinner party, only reinforced her belief that he would be better off with Selina.

Perhaps it was her own lack of self-confidence that made her feel so inadequate, she brooded. She'd come a long way since the days when she had been under Lee's spell. His mental cruelty had been a deliberate form of abuse, but even now that she was able to recognise it as such it had only taken a couple of meetings with him to shake her hard-won confidence.

She finally drifted off to sleep, but woke at dawn, alerted by the click of her door being opened. 'Who is it?' she whispered, her heart thumping erratically, and Alex muttered a rude word as he stubbed his toe on her bed.

'Father Christmas! Who else were you expecting to creep into your bedroom at the crack of dawn?'

'I wasn't expecting anyone,' she told him primly, her pulse-rate leaping when he drew back the covers and slid into bed beside her. 'I thought sex was off the menu while you struggle with a fit of nobility?'

'Don't tempt me,' he growled, and she couldn't prevent a blissful sigh as he drew her into his arms, his warmth and the tantalising scent of him pervading her senses. 'I didn't want you to wake up on Christmas morning feeling sad that Maisie isn't with you,' he confided huskily. 'I know you miss her, but we can still have a nice day, and we'll celebrate Christmas with her tomorrow.'

'That was a very kind thought,' Jenna assured him, her hands straying over his body as if they had a will of their own. 'I didn't think you wore pyjamas.'

'I am kind,' he told her, as he trapped her hand beneath his and moved it to an area of safety further up his body, 'and thoughtful, and patient.' He ignored her disbelieving snort. 'There's a very good reason why I'm wearing pyjamas—as you've just discovered,' he added on an indrawn breath, when her hand tugged free and continued its intimate exploration. 'Jenna, I honestly came here to comfort you, not to make love to you.'

'What a pity,' she murmured, with a heartfelt sigh that demolished his good intentions, and with one swift movement he rolled her onto her back and came down on top of her.

'I'm trying to do the right thing here,' he told her frustratedly, the humour in his eyes fading to be replaced with burning desire.

'I know,' she whispered. 'But, Alex, at this moment the right thing is to make love to me. I need you,' she admitted thickly, and he needed no second bidding, his mouth gentle at first, and then harder, demanding a response she was willing to give. She was on fire instantly, so ready for him that her nightdress was a hindrance swiftly removed along with his silk pyjama pants, and she sighed her pleasure at the first touch of his naked body on hers.

'Not this time,' he muttered, tugging her hand away as she closed her fingers around his throbbing shaft. 'Not unless you want this to be over in an embarrassingly short time.'

'I want you now,' she whispered, her thighs already parting to accommodate him, and with a muttered imprecation he entered her, swift and hard, driving into her with an urgency that betrayed him. As promised, it didn't last long, but for Jenna his savage loss of control filled her with a fierce exhilaration, and she revelled in her power even as he took her to the pinnacle of pleasure and tipped her over the edge.

From that moment the day became happier than she could possibly have expected. Of course she missed Maisie's excitement as the little girl unwrapped her presents—but she still had that to look forward to on Boxing

Day, she reminded herself, and the champagne breakfast Alex's mother served seemed the height of decadence.

She was stunned to discover that the majority of presents beneath the tree had her name on; it was a long time since anyone had surprised her with gifts, and she beamed her thanks to Alex as she unwrapped a range of top-quality art materials.

'I haven't given you much,' she confessed after lunch, when she found him studying the book on the history of aircraft that she had bought him, and he smiled, the warmth of his expression filling her with sudden hope.

'You've given me everything,' he said simply, leaning forward to take her mouth in a slow, sweet caress. It lasted long enough for his young nephew to mutter, 'Ugh— sloppy stuff!'

In the afternoon he gave her a tour of the village, and she curled her hand within his warm clasp, content to walk where he led. It was a small village, but they were out for a couple of hours as Alex insisted on stopping to kiss her at every vantage point, and it was growing dark when they finally returned to his parents' house.

'Oh, I'm glad you're back,' Katharine Morrell greeted them at the front door, and Jenna was instantly alerted by the older woman's concerned expression. 'Your ex-husband has rung twice. He says Maisie is unwell and he wants you to call him.'

'She was perfectly all right yesterday,' Jenna muttered worriedly as she dialled Lee's number. 'Hello, Lee. What's wrong?'

'Maisie's been sick all day,' came the terse reply, and she frowned, her mind hurtling through a mental medical dictionary.

'How sick? Is she running a high temperature?'

'What do you mean, how sick? I don't bloody know;

I've just spent most of the day scrubbing the carpet. Louise checked her temperature and it's up a bit. You'll have to come and collect her tonight; I can't cope with this for much longer.'

'It's probably just a combination of excitement and too many sweets,' Alex reasoned as Jenna flew about her bedroom, shoving her belongings into a bag, and the sensible part of her knew he was right, but at the same time a variety of dreadful diseases plagued her imagination.

'I won't be happy until I see her for myself,' she told him anxiously. 'I'll see if I can get a taxi, I don't want you to have to leave your parents and ruin their Christmas.'

'Don't be ridiculous. Of course I'll drive you over to collect her.'

'I'm sorry to spoil the evening,' Jenna apologised to Alex's parents as they waited in the hall while he stashed her bags in the car, and Katharine gave her a warm smile.

'It's been a pleasure to have your company for the day,' she assured her. 'But of course you must go and see to your little girl. I hope we'll see much more of you and Maisie in the future,' she added, and Jenna was aware of a complicated silent conversation between Katharine and her son, but was too concerned about Maisie to try and decipher it.

Lee was waiting with Maisie on the doorstep when they drew up outside the Love Nest, and Jenna jumped out of the car and snatched her daughter into her arms. 'Why are you standing out here in the cold? Do you want her to catch pneumonia?' she demanded.

'She's all right; just don't give her anything to eat or drink,' Lee muttered grumpily. 'Especially blackcurrant juice. She's ruined the upholstery in the sitting room; Louise has had to go and have a lie-down.'

'Maisie can't help being ill.' Jenna defended her daughter while Alex strapped her into the back of the car. 'Small children are prone to picking up viruses.'

'Yeah, well, it's been one hell of a Christmas, what with Maisie throwing up every five minutes and Louise's geriatric parents driving me mad. Her dad's as deaf as a post and her mother's got bad legs, apparently. She's had me running around after her like a skivvy.'

'Do I detect that all is not well in the Love Nest?' Jenna fought to hide the amusement in her voice.

'To be honest, I've had enough. Louise has got it into her mind that we could have a test tube baby.' Lee's face wrinkled in distaste. 'I'm not squirting my sperm into a damn test tube!'

'I understood that it was fairly crucial to your finances for you to marry her?' Jenna murmured, and Lee gave her an assessing look.

'How did you find that out, I wonder?' He glanced across at Alex, who was waiting impassively by the car, and sniffed. 'It seems the boyfriend is useful in more ways than one. I might need to disappear for a while,' he admitted. 'A few of the lads from the fire station have bought a bar in Spain and they want someone to go out and run it.'

'And they trust you?' Jenna's brows shot up. 'You can't possibly be hoping to take Maisie to Spain with you?'

'No!' A flash of horror crossed Lee's face. 'I've decided that she's better off with you after all.'

'Just like that?' Jenna shook her head in disgust. 'You can't just walk in and out of her life when it suits you.'

'I'll send her postcards,' Lee promised, and as Jenna recalled the weeks of worry he had caused, anger settled in her chest like a lead weight—cold and unforgiving.

'You'll do more than that,' she told him. 'You'll sign

a legal document waiving all claim to custody of her. I'll never stop you visiting her, if that's what you want, but you'll just have to take my word on it.'

'And if I don't agree?'

'Then I'll make sure your numerous creditors know exactly where to find you in Spain.'

As she walked down the front steps she felt Lee jostle her—nothing too obvious, but enough to make her stumble, and she gripped the wall to prevent herself from falling.

'Sorry,' he murmured, not bothering to disguise his sly grin, and she turned to face him, her contempt so palpable that the grin faded.

'Don't ever try and hurt me again,' she said, in a cold, clipped tone. 'I'm not afraid of you any more, Lee. I've finally seen you as you really are—weak and pathetic. The game's over,' she informed him as she walked across to the car, 'and I've won.'

She was shaking when she climbed into the car, the mixture of fear and elation that she had finally broken free from Lee causing her heart to pound. But several minutes passed and still Alex didn't join her.

'Alex, I think we should get Maisie home.' She walked around the side of the house and gasped when she found Lee lying in a crumpled heap in a puddle while Alex stood over him, his fist raised. 'No! Alex, stop—this is not the way to settle things,' she cried, hurrying across and standing between the two men. 'Leave Lee alone, please,' she begged. 'I don't want this.'

'I haven't even touched him yet,' Alex mocked disgustedly. 'I was simply demonstrating the ease with which accidents can occur—but then you know all about accidents, don't you, Deane?'

'Oh, God, Lee—are you hurt? Try and stand up,' Jenna

muttered as she knelt beside Lee and helped him to his feet.

'He attacked me for no reason,' Lee whined, quickly realising that for some reason he had Jenna's sympathy. He leaned heavily on her as he slowly stood up.

'He hurt you,' Alex growled, his expression so coldly furious that she shivered, and understood Lee's eagerness to move out of range. 'I saw the injuries he inflicted on you, the so-called accidents,' he continued bitterly. 'How can you possibly defend him?'

'You don't understand,' Jenna told him urgently, hiding her contempt for the way Lee was actually cowering behind her. She had Lee where she wanted him, he had agreed that he wouldn't fight for custody of Maisie, but if he was upset there was a danger he would change his mind and loom as an uncertain spectre on her horizon for ever. 'I just want to take Maisie home,' she whispered and as Alex slowly lowered his fist Lee drew himself upright.

'Yeah, you'd better clear off before I lose my temper.'

'Is that so?' Alex drawled as he strode over to the car, not even waiting for Jenna to fasten her seat belt before he fired the engine, and as he drove away his expression was so forbidding that she dared not say a word.

Maisie had fallen asleep, and the journey back to London was completed in a silence that crackled with tension.

An hour later they reached Jenna's house, but Alex still hadn't spoken, and she sighed as she carried Maisie upstairs, quickly washing her face and popping her into her pyjamas before the little girl fell back to sleep. In the living room she discovered that Alex had taken Maisie's presents from their hiding place in the cupboard under the stairs and arranged them beneath the tree, and she smiled softly as she imagined her daughter's face the next morning.

'Maisie will be so excited,' she murmured, but Alex's grim expression didn't flicker.

'I'm sure she will.'

'She'd like you to be here.' Jenna made the suggestion tentatively, unable to read Alex's mood and puzzled by his transformation from gentle lover to bitter antagonist.

'What about you, Jenna? Would you like me to be here?'

'Of course I would. How can you even ask?'

'Because I've realised tonight that I don't really know you at all—although I have discovered one rather salient fact that makes sense of everything else.'

'You're talking in riddles,' Jenna said, shaking her head. 'What fact have you discovered?'

'That you still have feelings for Lee. That you're still in love with him.'

For a few seconds Jenna was rendered speechless with shock, and when she did open her mouth it was to laugh. Alex was making some kind of joke, surely?

'Any feelings I have for Lee are unrepeatable,' she told him firmly. 'But if you're sulking because I stopped your fight, then too bad. You were in the wrong. Like a Neanderthal man. You're a barrister, for goodness' sake— you know the law; Lee could have you up for assault.'

'So you stopped me thumping him for my own good? Not because, despite everything he's put you through, you couldn't bear to see him hurt? He's been there right from the beginning,' Alex continued slowly. 'From the first day we met, when you let me believe you were still married to him. Why did you do that, I wonder? Was it because in your heart you wished it was the truth?'

'I've had enough of this,' Jenna snapped, her patience

at an end. 'You know why I lied about still being married to Lee; it was because I was so embarrassed by the overwhelming attraction I felt for you. Why don't you be honest?' she carried on, all the tensions of the past few hours spilling over. 'Having taken me to your parents' house, you've come to realise that I don't fit in your world. What am I, anyway, other than a single mother with a mountain of debts? We both know you would be better off with Selina— Where are you going?' she queried frantically as she followed him into the hall.

'Home,' he answered succinctly, his gaze travelling over her disparagingly, so that she was aware that her hair looked a mess and that she smelled faintly of sick from where she had carried Maisie upstairs.

'I thought you were going to stay,' she whispered, despising the note of pleading in her voice but unable to bear the thought of him leaving.

'I think not. You'll have to use a different sex toy tonight.'

She paled at the deliberate crudeness of his words, and stepped back, her hands falling helplessly to her sides. 'I'm not even going to try and answer that. Just go, Alex,' she told him bitterly when he turned in the doorway and she caught the hint of remorse in his eyes. 'I'll look for another job as soon as possible in the New Year. I think it'll be for the best for both of us.'

Maisie woke at dawn on Boxing Day, and demanded cereal and toast before she set to work on unwrapping her presents.

'I take it you're feeling better?' Jenna noted dryly. 'But I think it's a bit early in the day for chocolate.'

'Daddy was cross when I was sick,' Maisie confided, her smile fading for a moment. 'He said I was digstusting,' she added, struggling with the unfamiliar word. 'I'm not, am I, Mummy?'

'Of course you're not,' Jenna reassured her, and she determinedly pinned a smile on her face and welcomed her neighbours, Nora and Charlie, who were eager to share Maisie's Christmas.

Chris had invited his girlfriend for lunch, and by three o'clock everyone was relaxing after the big meal that Jenna had spent all morning preparing. Wearily she glanced around the room at the mound of wrapping paper and party hats, the tree that was doing a good impression of the Leaning Tower of Pisa and shedding needles all over the carpet, and sighed. Ideal home it was not, but it was her home, hers and Maisie's, and she refused to dwell on the fact that without Alex it felt as empty as her heart.

'I'll get it,' she murmured as the doorbell pealed. 'It's probably Claire from my old office; she said she might pop in.'

She opened the door to be met by a mass of red roses— at least three dozen, she estimated dazedly as her eyes moved up to meet Alex's sapphire gaze. She felt as if she was standing on the edge of a precipice. One wrong move could send her hurtling over the top. She fought to control the thunderous beating of her heart.

'I'm glad you chose something discreet and understated,' she said huskily, using humour to disguise her nervousness.

'Subtlety's my second name,' he agreed gravely, and her lips twitched. 'Alongside Neanderthal.'

'I can't believe I called you that.'

'I deserved it—and worse. I'm not usually quite so unpleasant,' he offered quietly and she read the sincere apology in his eyes, her smile decidedly wobbly as she stood aside to usher him in.

'I appreciate that you were defending me,' she said hurriedly, 'but Lee had just agreed not to apply for custody of Maisie, and I didn't want to give him a reason to change his mind. Alex, I'm really not in love with Lee,' she continued, desperate to clear up the misunderstanding before they were interrupted. 'I'm not sure I ever was. But I was young and had had a fairly sheltered upbringing. He was bold and daring, and my parents disapproved of him.' She shrugged. 'He swept me off my feet, and by the time I hit solid ground I was pregnant with Maisie. You can't seriously believe I have any feelings for him?' she pleaded.

She struggled to hold the huge bunch of roses. 'I think I'll have to put these in the bath for now; I've only got one vase. No one has ever bought me flowers before.'

'I'll buy you flowers every day,' Alex assured her gently, and he tilted her chin and brushed his lips over hers in a sweet caress that instantly had her clamouring for more. 'I don't want you to look for another job. The rather staid offices of Morrell and Partners haven't been the same since you burst through the doors, and neither have I,' he added, accepting the invitation in her eyes and deepening his kiss.

'Mummy, I need a cloth.' Maisie trotted into the kitchen and Jenna reluctantly pulled out of Alex's arms, frowning at the ominous request. 'Alex, I'm doing painting, but it's spilt on the cushion,' the little girl explained, beaming at Alex as he reached down to scoop her into his arms.

'We'd better clear it up, then, sweetheart, while Mummy finds somewhere to put her flowers.'

The rest of the day was a joyous hubbub of noise and laughter. Alex chatted to Nora and Charlie, and tried not to wince when Chris gave a demonstration on his electric guitar, and Maisie basked in his attention. As Jenna watched her daughter clamber unselfconsciously onto his knee she acknowledged that it was too late to try and build a defence barrier; Maisie adored Alex, and once again a frisson of fear curled around her heart.

One day at a time, Alex had advised about their relationship, and she was determined to do just that—no looking forward, no dwelling on the past; she would enjoy what she had today and let fate determine tomorrow.

She was unaware that Alex was watching her, reading the emotions that flitted across her face and feeling hope unfurl in his chest. Trust didn't come easily to her—not surprising after the way her ex-husband had treated her—but he had been patient; well, fairly, he conceded with a wry smile. He wasn't renowned for his patience, but as he caught her glance and watched the way her grey eyes darkened to the colour of woodsmoke a smile curved his lips and he contemplated the end of a very long journey.

It was late when Nora and Charlie returned to their own house. Chris decided to take his girlfriend on a tour of the local pubs, and Maisie was finally persuaded to go to bed. The house looked as if it had been blitzed, Jenna thought ruefully as she went downstairs, but in the living room Alex had switched off the overhead light, and the room looked cosy and romantic, bathed in the glow of the Christmas tree lights.

'I bet your flat never looks like this,' she quipped as she joined him on the sofa and accepted the glass of champagne he offered with a blissful sigh.

'Never,' he agreed. 'It's always felt rather sterile and unwelcoming—which is why I'm planning on buying a house. Aren't you interested to know which house?' he queried when she sat silent, staring at him with wide, expressive eyes over the rim of her glass.

'Which house?' she asked obediently, fighting her sudden feeling of panic. He wouldn't buy a house just for him—but surely he wasn't planning to marry Selina after all?

'The one next to the park. Maisie calls it the fairy house because she says it looks magical.'

'Well, that's nice. We'll practically be neighbours,' Jenna murmured, finding it suddenly hard to think coherently when his arm, which had been lying along the back of the sofa, settled around her shoulders and he pulled her close. 'That's odd—I didn't notice that there earlier,' she said, leaning forward to view a small package that dangled from a branch of the Christmas tree. 'Maisie must have forgotten to unwrap one of her presents.'

'Maybe you should open it,' Alex suggested softly as she stood in front of the tree, and her heart began to thump as she stared at the small parcel.

'You gave me my presents yesterday,' she reminded him as she pulled off the paper to reveal a small velvet box. It would be earrings, of course, or possibly a small pendant, she told herself, unable to prevent a gasp as she opened the lid and stared at the exquisite solitaire diamond set on a white gold band. 'Alex, I…'

He had been sitting quietly watching the play of emotions on her face, but now he came to stand behind her, wrapping his arms round her and drawing her against his chest. 'Marry me?' he begged, his voice muffled in her hair, but she caught the note of uncertainty, an almost vulnerable quality that turned her heart over.

'We've been through this before,' she began, unable to quell a delicious shiver as his lips caressed her ear, sharp teeth nipping the sensitive lobe before he trailed a line of kisses down her neck.

'And you told me that a marriage between us wouldn't work because we don't love one another.' He turned her in his arms so that she was facing him, and she stared at the male beauty of his face, shaken by the depth of emotion evident in his eyes. 'But that's not true—is it, my darling? I love you more than life, more than I believed it possible to love another human being. You are my world,' he murmured huskily, 'and you have been since the moment you fell into my arms in the storm. I think that deep down you care for me too. I know how badly Lee hurt you, and I can wait, and hope for your love to grow, but tell me you'll marry me. I need to know that I at least have the right to protect you and Maisie. I need to know you'll be there every day for the rest of my life.'

He looked like a man about to be sent to the gallows, Jenna thought through a mist of tears. He had said he was sure that she cared for him, but he wasn't that sure—she could tell from the rigid line of his jaw that he was struggling to keep his emotions in check.

'You don't have to wait,' she reassured him, stretching up to wind her arms around his neck. 'I think I've loved you for ever. You don't know how many times I nearly admitted that I was no longer married, but I was scared. I was sure you were only interested in a brief affair, and I had Maisie.'

'Meeting her for the first time was a shock,' Alex admitted with a rueful smile. 'But not because I don't like children. I hope we'll have half a dozen, and I love Maisie as if she was my own. You have no idea how badly you rocked my world that day. You looked so young and fragile, yet you were so determined to be strong for your daughter. I knew then that I loved you, although it took a mad dash down the motorway for me to accept my life was never going to be the same again.'

He didn't seem too sad about that fact, Jenna decided several minutes later as she lay on the sofa, her clothes scattered in a heap on the floor, quickly to be joined by his.

'Stop wriggling,' he admonished sternly as she entwined her legs with his, tilting her hips in her desperation to feel him inside her. 'This is the first time I've made love to you, knowing that you love me. I want it to last.'

'I've no problem with hard and fast,' she assured him, but by then she had no choice in the matter, and he drove into her, each powerful thrust sending her higher and higher, until she cried his name and clung to his shoulders while he found his own exquisite release.

'I thought we could have an extended honeymoon in New Zealand,' he murmured later, as they lay replete in each other's arms. 'It'll give your parents a chance to enjoy Maisie while I enjoy you,' he added throatily, and was rewarded with a smile that took his breath away.

'My parents will love you,' she said confidently, 'and Maisie already adores you. But their feelings fade to nothing compared to my love for you. You are my other half for the rest of my life; friend, lover and husband—for ever.'

HARLEQUIN *Presents*

Coming Next Month

HPCNM0606